THE RULES OF ENCHANTMENT

AN EROTIC FANTASY ADVENTURE NOVEL

WENDY TARDIEU

ISBN: 978-1-63161-083-7

Published by TCK Publishing
www.TCKpublishing.com

Get discounts and special deals on our best-selling books at
www.TCKpublishing.com/bookdeals

Sign up for Wendy Tardieu's newsletter at
www. wendytardieu.com/newsletter

Table of Contents

<h1>CHAPTER ONE</h1>

THE MESSAGE

The view was especially macabre in winter. Headmaster Wickham looked out over the balcony at the dying landscape: the misshapen black blemish at the bottom of the hillside was always there, marking the haunted forest he so often watched, and while the shoreline beyond was shrouded in morning fog, he could still hear the waves crashing violently against the cliffs. There was a knock on the door of his study, the carving of the Academy Arms still visible in its antique oak despite its faded, gnarled surface. He stepped back inside, twisting the end of his long, tapered white beard.

"Come," the old man barked.

A young man entered, nervous and thin with brown hair tied back tightly. His robes were similar to Wickham's—blood red, signifying the Order of Sight—but lacking the many embroidered runes and emblems his superior wore. He closed the door behind him and stood before the headmaster.

"You wished to see me," the young man reminded shakily.

"We have a dilemma, Rowan," Headmaster Wickham announced, as he took a seat in an ornate chair, the arms tipped with gargoyles. "One of our students has come to me with a disturbing vision," he said. "He says he has dreamt that someone will try to reclaim the Gauntlet of Malantheus."

The young man laughed at this. "Forgive me, my lord, but that's impossible," he said. "Malantheus is buried at Lamentiose, the most well-guarded and deeply enchanted island in all of Salyndria. His gauntlet is buried with him."

"And Lamentiose is only a few miles beyond that fog," the headmaster continued, gesturing toward the balcony. "We, of course, built the Chamber of Sight very near to it so that any ill adventures may be detected, but there are powerful sorcerers living there who can defend themselves against all four of our Orders."

"And whom does this student's vision suspect, Headmaster?" Rowan asked.

The old man's black eyes drifted to the view outside. There was a grave look in them as they peered out from under thick, white brows. "Master Leith, of Solemn Woods," came the words in a sinister whisper.

Rowan recoiled, took a step back, and awkwardly stumbled into a chair. He steadied himself, then cleared his throat. "Master Leith," he murmured, the simple mention of the name making him uneasy. "He has lived alone in the old forest observatory for four years now. He still serves the Order of Shadow. He knows he couldn't possibly get away with—"

"Leith was twenty-six when he was discharged from his chamber for dabbling in advanced spells," Wickham reminded him. "But the Academy has never seen a more powerful, nor a more ambitious, student. We needed his alliance, so we offered him a solitary place of study. He chose the observatory. There is no telling what he has been up to these years, and so close to the island."

"What must I do, Headmaster?" asked Rowan, suddenly dutiful and determined.

"You have an acquaintance," Wickham began. "One of our scribes. She studies the archives at the Chamber of Shadow."

"Kyler?"

"Yes. She began as a student, but never fully developed her craft. She has become a very useful historian, but I think it is time she revisited the study of magic."

"I'm afraid I don't understand," Rowan confessed.

"Every master of his Order is required to take one apprentice every two years. Master Leith has had the luxury of evading this decree twice. He was notorious at the Chamber of Shadow for making spineless, frightened worms out of his pupils, who always ended their first terms in the headmaster's quarters on their knees, begging to be transferred." Wickham's lip curled with amusement. "Since his isolation, we have not required him to take any students. But the more time he spends alone with his magic, the more he becomes a potential threat to us. He needs a distraction."

"You mean to send Kyler as his apprentice?" Rowan deduced in disbelief. "But, Headmaster, why not send me instead? Why not send our officers after him right away?"

"Because Leith is not an imbecile!" Wickham shot back. "He'll have any evidence of his ploy vanished before we set our horses out. We have no proof, and we have no right to invade his personal sanctum of study. The last thing we need now is to lose his allegiance. We'll send the girl. Though her magic is poor, she is intelligent—and loyal. If she suspects anything amiss, she will inform us."

"Then why did you call me, my lord?" Rowan said with his teeth clenched.

"She will need convincing, I think," Headmaster Wickham answered in a sigh. "Kyler obeys her Order without question, but apprenticeships are optional. Leith has a reputation, and she will not be quick to agree. She is a historian, after all, and must know the story behind Solemn Woods as well. It is not a place she will be eager to visit. You must persuade her."

"I think it best that I go in her stead, my lord. She is ill-equipped for such a . . ."

"You are trying me, Rowan," Wickham cut in. "Leith will have you licking your own vomit from the floor for his personal enjoyment. He will detect you immediately and torment you accordingly. Kyler knows nothing. She will have nothing to hide from him, and she will not provoke him with pride or arrogance."

"And she is beautiful," Rowan added reluctantly.

Wickham halted, then smiled. "Leith is obsessed with his magic. But he is a man, after all. An apprentice is a distraction—but a lovely one may be far more effective. I have sent a missive to the Chamber of Shadow requesting her. She will arrive tomorrow. You'll see her," Wickham commanded. "You may go."

Rowan swallowed, then exhaled. "Yes, Headmaster," he said, and turned.

"Rowan," said Wickham, stopping him. "Be grateful you weren't chosen to be the messenger to Solemn Woods, to inform Leith of his—" Wickham paused—"obligation."

Rowan swallowed again, nodded, and disappeared.

The emissary hesitated as he read the words, carved deep into the massive oak that guarded the entrance to the gloomy forest. It was the last ordinary tree before the outskirts of Solemn Woods, the flank beyond marked by smooth, coal-colored trees that stretched upward more than twenty feet. Their thin, crooked branches reached out like crippled fingers; the wind sounded like slow wheezing as it passed between them.

The man sat up straight, smoothed back a lock of blond hair, and gripped the reins of his horse, gently urging the animal onward. He wore the brown robes of the Academy's scribes and messengers, having not yet earned the dark green hem and sleeve bands of a scholar.

A cold shade fell over the path before him, a slender trail leading into the woods and vanishing into shadow. There was a stillness about the forest. Except for the wind, there was no movement amidst the trees, no musical chirping or rustling of brush. The young emissary pulled his hood over his head as his horse stepped warily onto the trail and the black trees closed in around him. Instantly, the daylight seemed to vanish, and the only light that guided him was a soft, noxious blue glow that seemed to come from the ground itself.

"I carry only a message," the boy whispered into empty air. "I mean no harm."

He stared ahead down the trail, a long, snaking path overgrown in some places, and crossed by black roots. There were voices in the woods, whispers and weeping that echoed in every direction. He would not look to his left or to his right, for there the spirits appeared between the trees, desperate to be mourned by the living. His horse was clearly uneasy as he made his way along the trail, exhaling into the winter air as he carried the boy deep into the heart of the forest. Finally, the tall gate that closed in the old observatory came into view. It reached halfway up the skeletal tree branches and ended in jagged spires.

The ancient gate was weatherworn and creaked in the cold wind; beyond, the land was thick with dried weeds that reached out from black earth. There were ruined garden statues of the older gods, their limbs and faces crumbling from centuries of weather and wear. There was a blue haze hanging low on the grounds, and from it rose the massive estate, a great shadow of a building with a tall dome atop its central tower, which now shone a light from its window. Distracted for only a second, the emissary made the mistake of turning his head to glance at something that moved in the woods. It was a white figure, stark against the black trunks of the trees—a woman with long, blonde hair and closed eyes, standing with her arms at her sides.

But she'd vanished in the same instant that she'd appeared.

The emissary held his breath, only half-certain he'd seen her, but desperate to move on before the apparition returned. He fixed his eyes on the gate, his steaming breath coming quicker as he neared it. He could hear someone weeping, but he kept himself from looking again. It sounded so near, like someone walking alongside his horse. He reached the gate and hurriedly dismounted. His shoulders hunched and his eyes wide, he did not dare glance behind him into the heart of Solemn Woods. He quickly clutched the reins and wrapped them around the gate's rusted bars, securing his horse. As soon as he turned, the woman's pale face whipped into view.

He leapt backward, crying out in alarm. Her eyes were open, the blood-red irises staring straight at him. Her blonde hair was damp and stringy, and her skin was like that of a corpse. She sneered suddenly, revealing a mouth full of blackened teeth.

"Beware the face of Solemn Woods!" she hissed as she lurched toward him.

The emissary stepped back and cried out once more, while the horse stirred and pulled at the reins, snorting wildly. The woman disappeared again, and the weeping turned to soft, mocking laughter that echoed through the trees behind him. The young man steadied himself, swallowed, and slowed his breathing. The horse was not so easily calmed; he continued to resist his bindings despite his rider's best efforts to ease him.

"Mitigo!" he commanded, with a short wave of his hand over the horse's eyes.

The horse ceased his movements as his huge head drooped. The emissary cinched his cloak at his neck and eyed the gate nervously; it creaked open with a gentle shove, and he was soon stepping across the withered, wasted grounds toward the front entrance of the estate. The building was nearly three quarters the size of the Chamber of Sight, made of dark gray stone with various carvings of moons, stars, and celestial guardians on the molding. There were four columns arranged in a half circle at the top of a wide staircase leading up to the doors, which were thick coated oak and bordered by sturdy iron straps.

There was a carving in the wood, centuries old: a circle with a seven-pointed star at its center. The young man recognized it as the symbol of Nythos, god of the night sky. The emissary reached up for the iron knocker and gave it a reluctant pound. The hollow sound echoed, and the light in the tower window seemed to flicker. He waited, looking up at the grandiose architecture and shuddering at the thought of making his way back through the woods.

There were footsteps, heavy and steady coming from inside. The boy stepped back as the sound of iron locks being tampered with alarmed him. Then he heard a deep, steady voice obscured by a harsh rasp.

"Impelium," the voice said from behind the door.

The boy was familiar with the word: it was an advanced spell that moved heavy objects. Suddenly, there was a great rumbling, and the oak doors swung open smoothly. Torches burned on both sides of the doorway, and a figure stood between them. He wore the black robes of the Order of Shadow: the silver borders on the hem and sleeves indicated that he was a Master of his Order. His hair was the same coal color of the trees, with loose black tresses nestled about his ears and neck and swept to one side of his forehead. His eyes were a piercing, almost luminescent light blue set in a princely young face. The emissary suddenly remembered a rumor that Master Leith had enchanted his own eyes, allowing him to see even in total darkness.

"What do you want?" the sorcerer intoned.

The boy looked up at the Master's face. It was pale and brooding, despite gently angled features and mournfully sloped black brows. The boy's words got caught in his throat as his mouth struggled to form a greeting.

"I have a message, my lord," the boy finally quaked, digging out the scroll from his robes and thrusting it outward. "From the Chamber of Sight."

"Oh . . ." Master Leith heaved a disappointed sigh and snatched it. The sorcerer examined the wax seal with discerning blue eyes. "How I look forward to these."

The boy suddenly jumped, startled as a low murmur exhaled in a cold breath on his neck. He whirled to look behind him, but there was nothing except the grim expanse of the observatory yard.

"Is there something wrong?" Leith asked, his voice slithering into the youth's ears.

"I thought I . . . I felt . . ." the boy stuttered. "Nothing, my lord. These woods lend themselves to madness."

"Yes," Leith agreed, straightening his posture and lowering the scroll to his side. "This land is soaked with madness," he said, and took a small step toward the young man.

The emissary cowered as he glanced up at the face once more, its pale, smooth features seeming to change before him. He was horrified as he watched the cheekbones slowly submerge, the skin sucked inward. The serious black brows began to turn gray, and the hair on his head gradually started to dry out into thin white strands.

"My lord," the boy choked out, stepping back. "You are afflicted!"

"Am I?" the sorcerer asked, putting a hand on his chest and glancing down at his black robes. "I feel very well, indeed," he said, the skin on his hands rapidly decaying.

"Please," urged the emissary, raising a hand to halt him as he backed down the stairway. "You must seek a remedy, my lord! This is the darkest kind of magic!"

"I have visitors so rarely," Leith said nonchalantly, his comely lips recoiling over a set of perfect teeth and his eyes retreating into his skull. "Won't you come in?"

The boy gasped in terror, then raced down the steps and across the yard to his dozing horse. He woke the animal roughly, mounting it just as it stirred from slumber and kicking him to a gallop. The horse tore off down the trail, whinnying as it carried the frightened young man back toward the edge of the woods.

Master Leith was satisfied. Smiling to himself, he withdrew into the torch-lined hallway.

"Impelium Restorai," he murmured with his back to the great ancient doors.

They rumbled behind him, drifting shut with an echoing boom. Leith paused, standing firmly on a circle of etched markings on the floor. Then, in an instant, the sorcerer vanished with a sound that resembled a heavy sack dropping to the ground, leaving only a light cloud of metallic dust in his wake as the torches continued to flicker.

He reappeared in a different room altogether, that same sound reverberating off the smooth walls, and the same cloud of dust rising up from his robes. An identical set of markings to those on the floor lay under his boots, and he stepped out of the circle while looking down at the scroll in his hands. The room was high in the tower and cluttered with jars and spell books, archaic containers that sat over a flame, the liquid bubbling inside. There were tall shelves that housed more books and baubles, a crow's skeleton in suspended flight mounted on a thick wooden base, ornate boxes carved from bone, and jars full of feathers and talons.

An old woman sat hunched at a table in the far corner. She wore a faded red robe trimmed with gold borders and nearly a dozen dangling necklaces and charms, and over all that lay the gossamer drape of her long white hair. She had a wrinkled face that might have once been beautiful, but was now obscured by the absence of one eye, the blank skin in its place crossed by a scar. When she spoke, her voice was like an unoiled hinge.

"You used a glamour on the poor boy," she said, not looking up from her runes.

"He'll recover," said Leith dryly, breaking the wax seal.

"He'll have nightmares for weeks," the old woman replied, her one eye drifting his way and a smirk lifting her wrinkled mouth.

"Let's hope," Leith returned, opening the scroll and reading it. The luminescent blue eyes glided over the words, and he grimaced suddenly. "That insolent wretch," he hissed, reading further. "He wants me to take an apprentice."

The old woman cackled and gathered up the runes in her hand. "Headmaster Wickham is no fool," she remarked. "You didn't think he'd leave you to your devices forever, did you?" she asked, taking up a vial of green powder and tossing some onto the runes in her hand.

"This will be short-lived," said Leith, his eyes narrowing into devious slits. "I'll send the little mouse scurrying out of Solemn Woods faster than that perfumed herald." He waved a hand at the window that looked down onto the grounds.

Instead of replying, the old witch opened her hand, pitching eleven small wooden blocks onto the table surface before her. She sucked in a deep breath and blew the powder from them, which caused a cloud of green dust to rise into the torchlight.

"No," she squeaked, touching them gently with the tip of her rotted fingernail. "You must follow through with this one, my lord," she said gravely.

"What is this madness you speak?" Leith asked. "I won't tolerate a blundering young student snooping around the observatory," he said. "He's bound to delay our new project."

"Your new apprentice is not a he," the witch answered. "Wickham sends you a diversion, a young girl. He knows we are up to something."

"Of course," Leith agreed, crossing the room to another table where a carafe of wine and a goblet rested. He poured himself a drink. "My spells of concealment could only deter the Chamber of Sight for so long. It was only a matter of time before they foresaw a disturbance."

"You must teach her," the witch advised, reading the runes. "If you scare her away, Wickham will only send another. The faster she earns her robes, the sooner we can get back to work. And it will be years before the Academy can insist you take another student," she told him, then blew on the runes again.

She was quiet a moment, staring at the blocks as though a face were peering back at her.

"What is it?" Leith asked, taking a long sip from his goblet.

The old witch paused. "The girl . . . may be of some use to us. But there is danger. Something . . ." The old woman coughed suddenly. "I can't see it!" she wheezed.

"By Nythos!" Leith snapped, bringing her the wine in his hand.

She took the goblet, sipped from it, and cleared her throat. "You must beware, my lord!" she whispered harshly. "She will tempt you. You must not let your magic suffer."

"Save your breath," Leith snarled, picking up one of the rune-blocks and turning it over with long, slender fingers. "I am not the brutish fool who chases the beautiful maid to the edge of the cliff. Don't insult me," he said, and chucked the rune back onto the table. "Let her come. We will have our amusement, yet."

The Chamber of Sight rested on a gentle hill overlooking the coast. The long path up to the wide front stair was neatly lined with tall Gentilium trees that blossomed throughout winter with hundreds of tiny, white, star-shaped flowers. The ground between was almost always covered with petals, but now they shared estate with the fallen snow. Rowan stood at the top of the grand staircase of the Chamber's entrance, watching as a figure came into view. He knew her horse, a strong and rugged animal with a brown coat and white patches on his flanks. The young rider was enveloped in a dark green cloak, her hands gripping the reins with what he imagined was just the right pairing of force and tenderness.

Rowan quickly smoothed his robes and perked his chin up. He rushed down the steps to greet her as she dismounted. A middle-aged stableman with curly black hair approached and took the reins from her.

"Lady Kyler," the man said with a nod.

"Hello, Hanover," she answered cheerfully, throwing back her hood.

Rowan swallowed the lump in his throat. Long, ribbon-like tresses of chocolate-colored hair spilled out down her shoulders, held together loosely in the back by a single fraying cord. Her smooth, fair complexion was made pink on her nose and cheeks by the cold. Her body under the cloak was layered in brown robes with green bands, the signature clothing of an accomplished scribe, and a beautiful silver medallion set in amber and emeralds peeked out from the neckline.

"Kyler," Rowan called out, his voice cracking.

The young woman turned. Her eyes, warm gold-green and rimmed by black curling lashes lit up at the sight of him.

"Rowan!" she exclaimed, and immediately embraced him. "Oh, it's good to see you. They told me to bring all my belongings—I think they wish me to stay awhile," Kyler began excitedly. "Headmaster Wickham wrote the summons himself, so it must be important, whatever they want with me."

Rowan remembered she'd had a birthday since he'd seen her last. She was twenty-one now, but her enthusiasm was always that of a child, eager to learn and explore, in wonderment of everything. Rowan listened as he ushered her up the stairs and marveled at her beauty.

Her face was marked by soft, kind features: a gently sloping nose, and smooth, gracefully shaped lips—but the eyes betrayed the rest. In her eyes there was strength—solidity. Rowan had never seen her doubt herself in any undertaking—save one. Kyler's struggle to prove her worth, both to the Academy and to herself, had always been something he saw beneath her cheerful demeanor as long as he'd known her.

"I finally finished archiving the Pyramon Rebellion," Kyler continued. "I studied the Treaty and all the sorcery-related murders that occurred before the regulations. Oh, listen to me!" she said, stopping at the top of the stairs. "I'm sorry to go on like that. I have been locked away at the Chamber of Shadow for months. I suppose all that time isolated in the mountains has made me desperate for conversation. The only place to get away was Storm Side, and you know what a grumpy town it can be once the rain turns to snow. They have to open the trenches, and that leaves just the one main road."

"It's all right," said Rowan swiftly, once the girl paused. "I want to hear everything once you're settled. But first, I want to tell you . . . I know why you were sent for."

Kyler's green eyes opened wide. "You know?" she asked, smiling. "What is it? What do they want of me?" She gasped suddenly. "They want me to chronicle the history of the Hypnogoths!" she whispered.

"No," Rowan said.

"I've always said the documents are hideously incomplete," Kyler went on, as though she hadn't heard. "The oldest creatures of our world deserve a proper and unbiased record. The ancient scribes depict them as sinister monsters, but I've been trying to . . ."

"Kyler," Rowan stopped her. "Headmaster Wickham wishes to reassign your studies."

Kyler halted, tilting her head in confusion. "To what?"

"To magic," said Rowan.

The young woman blinked. "What?" she replied in disbelief. The smile vanished, the beautiful lips turned downward, and the eyes looked past him. "He wishes me to study magic again? But why?"

"He has foreseen great things for you," Rowan struggled to say. "He believes you can be taught. He thinks you're ready." He smoothed back his hair again as Kyler looked away.

"I don't understand," Kyler murmured. "Why now, after five years? I've been a scribe since I was sixteen. You remember what a disaster my lessons were before you won your robes. Every master I had tired of me after the first term—or when they suffered injuries, whichever came first. I've tried so hard to prove my usefulness in the strengths I do have. I don't want to go back to a world where I always fail."

"But you have magic in you," Rowan persisted, trying to meet her eyes. "They placed you at the Chamber of Shadow when you were twelve. No one is assigned their Order so young."

"Rowan," she sighed. "The Order of Shadow's discipline is harmful and destructive spells. *Everything* I attempted caused harm and destruction. It just took them a little while to realize the effect was unintentional, and by then, there was nowhere more fitting to put me."

Rowan had no argument. Kyler moved toward the edge of the wall to gaze out at the hillside. Beyond her was the misted seacoast, the outline of jagged cliffs miles away.

"Who is to be my master?" the girl asked quietly, her gaze still on the sea.

Rowan swallowed again, his hands gripped together in front of him. "Master Leith," he choked out.

Kyler whirled, then stared at him. "What?"

"Master Leith," Rowan said clearly this time.

"Rowan, please don't jest," she blurted, her delicate brown eyebrows wrinkling in despair.

But the young man could only shake his head. "Headmaster Wickham has already sent him word that an apprentice will be arriving tomorrow."

"Tomorrow!" Kyler exclaimed, then quickly collected herself. "There must be some mistake. Master Leith, the retired assassin, agreed to teach sorcery to a scribe?"

"Assassin?" Rowan repeated with surprise.

"Leith was the kingdom's most valued. He was responsible for seizing the fortress at Pyramon after the other sorcerers fell to the guards," she told him. "The Order discovered later that the only reason he was able to accomplish it was because he'd used forbidden spells to give himself . . . *abilities*. They put him on trial. I was authorized to read the confidential archives."

"I . . . I knew he was discharged, but, I suppose the details of his crimes would make the Academy seem vulnerable if made fully known," Rowan began haltingly.

"This is absurd," Kyler remarked almost to herself, crossing her arms into the sleeves of her robes. "I have work back at my chamber. I don't wish to spend an entire term in those woods. The Order of Spirit has declared that land unclean. Evil lives in those trees. Malantheus's disciples were cursed by the Necromantis there. How can I learn anything in a place like that?"

Rowan hesitated, remembering the Headmaster's task. *Convince her.*

"You've always been fascinated with Malantheus's era," he began carefully. "Think of the history you could uncover living in the heart of an ancient landmark. And Master Leith," he continued. "Think of the stories he must have. Headmaster Wickham is one of the most powerful prophets alive. If he believes you can learn magic, imagine how it could change things for you—what Leith could teach you."

Kyler shook her head slowly. "I don't know," she said, tucking a strand of brown hair behind her ear. "I gave up on my magic long ago. I accepted my failure and found something I was truly skilled at. I don't want to give myself that hope again."

Rowan reached out a thin arm and placed it around her shoulders. "I have faith in you, Kyler," he said to her. "You should accept the apprenticeship."

Kyler patted his hand. Rowan briefly sighed, relishing her touch. "Tomorrow?" she sighed, shutting her eyes tight.

"There is a banquet tonight," Rowan said. "After you meet with Headmaster Wickham, there is a ceremony for those who have received their robes. You shall have one night of merriment before you set off for the observatory."

Kyler paused. "This will be an adventure, my old friend," she said.

CHAPTER TWO

THE ARRIVAL

The hall was decorated in rich, ruby-colored draperies, and the air within was warmed by torches fixed high on the walls. A banquet table was prepared, along with a large space in the center where people were dancing. There were musicians, bouquets of Gentilium flowers, and barrels of wine. Kyler stood in the doorway, wearing a long green gown with flared sleeves and a swooping neckline that complimented her medallion, the only family heirloom she owned that signified her ties to the priests of Amaleus, god of forgiveness and compassion. She had combed her long brown ringlets, pinning back the sides and letting the rest fall down her back. She looked over the scene with delight, but underneath lay apprehension that even the sounds of the festivities couldn't quiet.

It had been an uneasy conversation with the headmaster, and she was relieved that it was behind her. Kyler stepped into the room. It was difficult to accept the assignment with her usual sense of duty. From a young age, she wanted to be worthy of sorcery. She often thought that her mother's decision to bring her to the Academy was a mistake. But, the Headmaster assured her that this would be her chance to try again, even amid her doubts of her abilities. She had convinced herself that this new apprenticeship was a wonderful opportunity, and she would face it with courage. As she stepped into the room, several of the attendees paused to look at her, some even attempting a glance as they danced. She stopped at one of the barrels and poured herself a drink.

"There you are," Rowan said, appearing at her side.

"I'm late, I know," she replied, forcing a laugh as she brought the cup to her lips. "I'm afraid I've almost completely forgotten how to dress myself for occasion."

"You look beautiful," Rowan said quickly, before taking her free hand and kissing it. Kyler's brows knitted briefly at the gesture, but she forged a smile once he raised his head again. "Will you dance with me?" he asked her.

"Certainly," she said, reluctantly laying aside her still-full cup.

The musicians played a cheerful arrangement of lyre and flute as Rowan awkwardly led her across the floor. She followed him as best she could, trying not to laugh at his missteps. His clumsiness was an endearing quality to her; she had always thought of him as a brother. When the tune ended, the partners bowed to each other and applauded. Rowan excused himself, having seen one of his superiors wave him over. The boy frowned, trudging over and looking back at Kyler all the while. She was slightly comforted—Rowan seemed especially attentive since her arrival, and it distressed her, though she could not place why.

Her eyes then fell on the stable hand, Hanover, who was in the corner of the room sneaking away toward the kitchen with a smaller barrel of wine, no doubt to share with some more of the staff. It signaled a more informal celebration, likely away from the crowd. The idea appealed to her, having had more comfortable company with them over the years than with her fellow members of the Order. Spending most of her time alone in the archives had left her with little capacity for social formalities. She bit her lip, then raced over to where she had left her cup. Rowan seemed distracted for the moment, and so she attempted her escape. Kyler was arrested, however, by a red-haired chubby boy in red robes that stepped timidly into her path. He was about ten, with a face full of freckles and bright blue eyes.

"Yes, sir?" she asked him kindly.

The boy motioned for her to step closer to him. Kyler obeyed.

"You must tell him 'no'," the boy said in a shy whisper.

"Pardon?" Kyler returned.

"When he asks you, say 'no'. Don't say you'll think about it. Don't say you need time. It will make things easier."

"When who asks me what?" she asked.

The boy stared up at her, then turned and walked quickly away. Kyler blinked, shook her head, and took a sip from her cup. She wondered if he was talking about the headmaster. In that event, the boy's abilities were underdeveloped—she had already given her answer. Kyler watched him vanish into the crowd, then followed Hanover's trail.

The stables were bright with firelight, and Kyler's horse seemed happy to have her nearby. He put his snout through the opening for her to touch, and she stroked him gently while she sipped the last of her wine. Hanover and the other servants were gathered around the barrel, the sound of loud off-key singing echoing into the night. Kyler felt more at home, as scribes were often looked upon as servants more than sorcerers, after all.

> To Storm Side go the fishermen, to Tawdry Cape, the thieves,
> Where the river winds its way beneath enchanted eaves.
> Your lady friend has left your side, and up the mountain gone.
> You'll find another soon enough in wicked Pyramon!

"You've got the words, but not the tune," Kyler teased. "And don't blame it on the wine!" she added, quickly pointing at Hanover, who looked as if he were about to defend his singing.

She sat atop a stack of hay, her hair loose now and pulled behind one ear. She sang another verse with them and caressed her horse's neck, but the revelry was soon interrupted.

"Kyler!" a familiar voice shouted over the singing.

They all hushed and looked up. Rowan's thin figure stood at the stable doors. He must have called her name several times before resorting to yelling it. He cleared his throat, and the servants slowly disbursed. One gathered up the barrel and carried it away. Kyler hopped off the hay and walked over to him.

"What's the matter?" she asked, seeing the troubled look on his face.

"I was looking for you," he said. "I didn't know you'd come here."

"Pherylon always seems uneasy when we travel to this part of the kingdom. I think he can sense the woods nearby." She looked back at her horse, who neighed once. "I thought I'd come visit him."

"Perhaps Pherylon is ready for his red robes," Rowan remarked sarcastically.

The brown horse snorted at him. Kyler frowned again. "Are you all right?" she asked him, raising one eyebrow.

Rowan seemed to check himself. "Yes, I'm sorry. Some things on my mind, I suppose."

"Like what?"

"I'm worried about you studying with Master Leith," he said.

"After all, you will be alone with him much of the time and I'm afraid he would . . . would take advantage."

Kyler laughed softly. "You need not worry. I've heard about the curious young witches that venture into the woods for a chance to share his bed, but I am not one of those. Master Leith may take his lovers, but he is still a faithful servant of the Academy and wouldn't dare violate the code of apprenticeship, especially for someone like me. Besides, lust impedes magic, we all know that. Beyond the fact that a sorcerer of his stature wouldn't be interested in a scribe, do you think I would not protect my own virtue?" she added with a wounded voice.

"Of course I don't think that," Rowan answered quickly. "Such things are forbidden, and you are loyal to your Order." His words were almost rhythmic, as if he were reciting them.

Kyler had stepped away as he spoke, reaching up to examine the straps of her saddle. She was slowly wandering about the space, running a hand over the stable doors and touching the other horses on their noses. Rowan cleared his throat again.

"I was hoping we could speak about something," he said. "I was hoping . . ."

"What is it?" Kyler asked.

"Here at our chamber, we spend so much time trying to see the future of others," he began, again sounding as if he'd rehearsed his words. "Only rarely do we contemplate our own. But I've thought about my future, Kyler, and I've seen you in it."

Kyler froze, her pulse suddenly racing in her ears. "Rowan . . ." she started to say.

"We've known each other for a very long time," he went on nervously. "I've always felt that we have a connection. From the moment we met, when Wickham asked you to help me in documenting my research for my classes, I knew we were meant for each other. All those long talks in the library over our books made me feel like we were the only people in the world. I'll die if I let you out of my sight again without telling you how I feel. I love you," he said. "I want you to marry me."

Kyler's eyes rounded in alarm. Her body froze, unmoving next to the stable doors. She had mistaken his affection for her in all their moments of confidence. She considered him family, something she never truly had, and put all her trust and comfort in him, not realizing he was developing feelings for her. Kyler had never been in love, but she knew it wasn't what she felt for Rowan. The silence was broken by a loud snort of protest that came from Pherylon's stall. Kyler jumped, putting her hand to her chest. Tell him you'll think about it, she told herself, but she didn't speak. The red-haired boy's freckled face came back to her, and she looked up at Rowan, studying the gaunt young man who had been her classmate long ago.

"I'm sorry, Rowan," she said. "You are a dear friend to me, but not more."

Rowan blinked. "You don't feel anything for me?" he asked, puzzled. "But I thought . . . don't you think you should take some time? Surely the wine—"

She shook her head firmly. "With or without the wine, my answer is no."

There was silence again. Rowan stood there a moment. He nodded in understanding, and a hurt look crossed his face. He bowed and turned away from her, vanishing into the night before she could even cry out after him.

The morning arrived quickly. Kyler had gotten very little sleep since the previous night's events, and hastily packed her things. It was now a relief that her assignment was the next day. She wanted so desperately to get away that she said her farewells to just a few friends before setting off down the path early. Though it pained her, she avoided a farewell with Rowan, dodging all his usual haunts and study spaces. She felt it might be better for them to spend some time away from each other, and she didn't want one more awkward encounter to distract her from what she was about to face.

Pherylon stopped in front of the great oak, stomping his hooves and bobbing his head up and down. Kyler huffed after urging him several times to move forward. She dismounted. Her bags were hung about his spotted flanks, and she was bundled in layers under her brown robes. Her favorite pair of wolf-skin traveling boots touched the ground, which was half-covered in morning snow.

"This is not up for negotiation," Kyler told her horse, pulling on his reins. He wouldn't budge. "What's the matter?" she said, placing one hand on her hip. Pherylon snorted, then nodded his snout at the ominous opening of the woods. Kyler followed his beady-eyed gaze. "Yes, I know," she said. "Do you think I'm happy about this? Do you think I want to take that trail any more than you do?" She jerked her thumb at the border of black trees in front of them. "We're in this together, whether you like it or not. You don't have to carry me: we'll walk together, but you're going in there. Unless you'd like to spend an entire term at the Chamber of Sight with Rowan looking after you."

The horse blinked, then finally quieted. Kyler gave the reins a tug and Pherylon stepped forward. She nodded to herself. Girl and horse entered Solemn Woods, and the daylight faded as the trees closed in around them. Kyler led her horse slowly along the narrow trail. The wheezing wind passed through the smooth black branches, and the blue glow hovered low on the ground. Kyler's heartbeat quickened, and her green eyes were steadfast on the trail. The temptation to inspect the rest of the forest around her was strong, as she had studied the woods but never set foot in it. Strange and haunting sounds whirled all around her, and her scholarly instincts drove her to search for their source. Pherylon complained with soft neighing. She took her hand from her cloak and smoothed his mane as they walked.

"I don't like this any more than you do," she told him.

Suddenly, out of the corner of her eye, she spotted a white figure flitting from behind one tree to another with what sounded like an echoing whisper. Kyler shut her eyes until the urge to look subsided. The whispering grew louder and seemed to merge with a second voice, as if in conversation. Some she could make out, like "Who comes?" and a mocking "She must be lost."

"Let her pass," Kyler thought she heard one of them say. And then, ". . . medallion."

She reached under her robes to touch the silver circle, her fingertips running over the smooth protruding gemstones. With more confidence, she clasped her cloak closed again and led Pherylon at a faster pace. Finally, the huge gate loomed before her, bordered by black branches like charred fingers gripping it from either side. Kyler peered up at the bleak observatory, the dome peeking just above the canopy of trees and catching only a wisp of daylight. She wrapped her fingers around one of the rusting bars and pushed open the gate.

She took the horse with her over the weed-ridden grounds, her boots surrounded by that eerie blue glow as she walked through the mist. There were the whispers, still, only they sounded distant now, as if their masters would not trespass the gate. Kyler gazed up at the huge doors, each marked with the symbol of Nythos. She gathered her courage and wrapped Pherylon's reins around a nearby statue. He followed her toward the stairs until his bindings pulled him back, whinnying in dismay.

"It's all right," she told him, then continued up the steps.

Kyler took a deep, icy breath and used the knocker. It made an echoing boom, like a distant crack of thunder. She waited. The voices in the woods kept up their whispers, snake-like and anxious, but she refused to turn toward them. She marveled at the corroding facade, with its symbols and carvings. She recognized the figures, old, forgotten gods she'd studied on scrolls, stored deep in the Chamber of Shadow's archives. The observatory's dome loomed above her, a place where scholars once watched the sky. Now, it echoed with a faint shrieking. She knew the sound well—the entire dome had to be full of bats.

"Impelium," a low, hoarse voice commanded.

Kyler jumped back from the doors as they began to move. Firelight pierced the shadows and the ghostly blue haze. Torch flames came into view first, before the figure of a man, tall and brooding, appeared in front of her. She stared up at him: pale blue eyes stared back, half-closed, regarding her with little interest. He was partly lit by the flames, his overgrown night-colored hair falling in careless tresses about his forehead and neck, his strong black brows angled as if in perpetual distress.

"Master Leith," Kyler surmised, noticing with awe how the eyes peering into hers glowed as though by their own power.

The man took a small step toward her. His long black robes nearly touched the ground, and silver rings on almost every slender finger peeked out of a silver-trimmed sleeve, catching the torch light. He looked her over, then exhaled with disappointment.

"Tell the head of your Order," he said to her, withdrawing back into the doorway, "I am unavailable for interviews. The Chamber of Shadow has all the records of my past they'll ever need. I don't narrate the Rebellion for scribes or anyone else," he said in his rasping voice.

"But, Master Leith, I'm not—"

"It's admirable that you braved these woods for the sake of history, but I only accommodate one kind of uninvited guest. And," he paused, cocking an eyebrow at her worn cloak and windblown hair, "they are usually better ornamented."

"I'm your apprentice, my lord," she blurted after him, just as he vanished from view.

She waited only seconds, relieved she had not heard the counter spell that closed the door. The man's face reappeared, eyes narrowed in suspicion. He looked her over a second time.

"What?" he said at last.

"I'm Kyler. I'm to be your apprentice for the new term," she told him.

"Why are you dressed as a scribe?" he asked her.

"I am a scribe, my lord."

Leith hesitated. Then his astonishment gave way to a sneer, and he laughed wickedly. "Forgive me," he said.

"Have they told you nothing about me?" Kyler asked.

"Nothing at all," Leith returned, still laughing. "What Order do you serve, girl?"

Kyler frowned at this address. "The Order of Shadow," she said.

"Well, that's a start," said Leith. He then looked over her shoulder at Pherylon, who was still tied to the statue. "He's yours?"

"Yes," she answered.

"He will stay in the courtyard. There is an old stable there. He'll be fine tied up for a few moments while I show you around. You can come back for him. Come inside," Leith commanded, and motioned for her to follow him.

Kyler stepped through the doorway between the torches and into the warmth beyond. The walls were lined with more torches that illuminated faded tapestries of star charts and runes. She pulled back her hood, watching Master Leith's tall, slender form glide away from her, the silver striped hem of his robe trailing behind him.

"Impelium Restorai," he said, not looking back.

The doors closed behind her. And then, suddenly, Leith disappeared with a loud popping sound, a cloud of metallic dust replacing him.

Kyler stopped in her tracks with a yelp of alarm. She checked the hall frantically, squinting in the dim light in an attempt to see its shadowed end. Bewildered, she waited, wondering if it wasn't some kind of prank. The sorcerer certainly didn't seem happy to see her. She soon noticed a crude etching on the ground, a circle of runes and shapes gleaming in the light. After closer inspection, she recognized the markings: a transport conduit, something only masters of their orders were allowed to use.

Seconds later, Leith reappeared in the same manner in which he'd vanished. Kyler cried out and stepped back as the flames danced in their sconces.

"Apologies," he said dryly, brushing off the dust. "It's a habit I suppose I should break for now," he added resentfully. "I'll show you the way." He turned on his heel again, and Kyler reluctantly followed him toward another pair of doors at the end of the hall, which he opened to reveal a large main room.

"Orb," he uttered.

The Master cupped one hand, holding it out palm-upward in front of him. A small, glowing sphere of soft white light materialized just above it. The light revealed a massive fireplace at one end, and several tables and chairs, some overturned, along the sides. There were four windows overhead, which let in only a shred of dusty daylight. There were murals hanging from the rafters, torn at the ends and discolored from age. There were bookshelves loaded with charts and journals, looking as if they hadn't been touched in centuries. Leith moved forward, holding the light in his hand as he walked.

"The kitchen," he told her, waving his free hand at an archway to her right. "The library," he said, indicating a passageway that led off to the left.

She followed him across the room to the fireplace, where a narrow staircase made its home in the adjacent wall. The stairs curved upward and were lost behind the stone. As Leith ascended them, Kyler trailed behind, lifting her brown robes as she climbed each step. It occurred to her that not only was it likely he never used the staircase, but that he didn't need the light, either. His orb illuminated carvings on the rounded wall: symbols of Nythos, crows, bats, and decorative etchings. They passed a small window that looked out over a small, weed-ridden courtyard.

Though the staircase continued to curve up to another floor, Leith stopped at the first archway. He extinguished the light by closing his hand over it. Kyler was relieved to see that the wide hallway that greeted her was alight with torches. There were doors in sequence on the right and left, and the end opened up into another large room where she glimpsed what looked like a laboratory. There were tall bookshelves, a long table with jars and instruments, and a huge window on the back wall with a thick curtain drawn halfway.

"The astronomers' quarters," Leith explained, nodding at the doors that lined the hall. "I've prepared one for you—the last door before the laboratory. The privy is just across from that. My quarters are upstairs in the tower," he added severely, the tone in his hoarse voice indicating that the tower was off-limits. "Breakfast and dinner are served promptly at sunrise and sunset. Any other meals you wish to have, you'll make yourself," he said, turning to face her. "We begin our lessons at midday. I suggest you take the time beforehand to prepare for them. I am not a patient teacher and I do not care for idleness. You'll do as I instruct and you won't question my instructions. Is this understood?"

Kyler met his gaze. "Yes, Master Leith," she answered.

There was a hint of surprise in the serious blue eyes, fixed on her as if she were a troublesome rodent he was forced to share a cage with. Perhaps he expected her to recoil and stutter.

Perhaps he was hoping she would.

"Let's see to your horse," Leith advised after a moment. "He can be led into the courtyard through the garden passageway out front. I am not a stable hand, so you'll care for him yourself."

"Yes, Master Leith," she said again.

Leith led her back downstairs without saying more, then opened the door with his spell.

Kyler poked her head outside, where Pherylon was still tied up.

"I'll wait for your knock," he said curtly. "And don't take all day."

She took a step toward her horse before turning back. "But, master, what about my—"

She was about to ask him for help with her things, but his low voice quickly said, "Impelium Restorai!" and the door rumbled shut again.

Kyler flinched at the sound, then looked cautiously around. She approached Pherylon and took his reigns.

"Let's go, boy," she said, untying him.

She led him to a wrought iron gate at the side of the front entrance. It creaked as she pushed it open. The courtyard was rectangular in shape, closed in by the east wing of the observatory. What might have once been a beautiful and flourishing garden was now a sprawl of dead weeds and broken cobblestone walkways. Kyler glanced up at small windows dotting the walls that loomed up around her, one set in a cylindrical stone tower attached to the larger building, which housed the dome. It was the window she looked down from only moments before.

"It's very cheery, isn't it, Pherylon," she remarked.

She walked him toward the hollowed stall that was to be his stable. The courtyard entrance bore an inadequate iron gate at the end of a long outdoor corridor. The ground was icy, so Kyler stepped carefully across the yard. There was a well, a cold drum made up of round stones that stood at half her height in the center of the walkways. Pherylon stuck his snout in it briefly, but the well was bone-dry (and had been for years, by the looks of it).

It was a deep, dark void with no reflection to behold. She tried to see its bottom, staring hard at the distant black circle, her eyes working out the shadows. Voices in the woods echoed suddenly. There was laughing, then footsteps. Startled, she backed away from the well and walked Pherylon to his new home. The stall wasn't large, but it would suit him. It looked as if her master had provided the minimum: a few bales full of food and some buckets of water. She hurried to unsaddle him and gather up her bags. She gave him a few pats of reassurance and made sure he was secured in the stall. Hoisting her bags over her shoulder, she made her way back to the door.

She knocked timidly, but got no response. The thought occurred to her that after meeting her, he'd decided to lock her out for good.

"Master?" she called.

Another moment passed. She looked around, feeling a brief sense of panic. Finally, his voice came. The door opened, and he stood on the threshold, looking annoyed.

"I believe I said I don't have all day," he muttered.

"Sorry, Master."

He stepped aside to let her back in. Leith muttered the spell to close it again.

"I assume you have a light spell?"

"Of course."

"Good," he said. "Use it to find your way back to your room. I have things to attend to. Get yourself settled and meet me in the laboratory. You'll need to orient yourself to our workspace."

He turned, disappeared into the conduit, and left her there in the empty entryway, loaded with her affects.

"Lovely to meet you," Kyler grumbled, and called her flame to light the way.

It was a laborious climb up the stairs until she was finally at her room again. The door creaked open and the young apprentice entered, the firelight from the hall pouring in with her. She coughed and put one sleeved arm under her nose, waving the dust away with the other. Once it settled, the room revealed itself: It was small, a neatly made bed with a curtained canopy against the wall, a barren writing desk in the corner, and a table with a candleholder by the door. Above her there was a cobwebbed chandelier. To her right against the wall was its long lighting wand.

Next to the desk was a narrow bookshelf, empty except for outlines of dust. It was clear her master wished to keep her undistracted. Kyler was disappointed—it would have been a treat to read through the previous occupant's journals. It occurred to her then that she was likely the room's first guest in hundreds of years. She coughed again and removed her cloak, carefully placing it over the desk chair. She recognized its design immediately: the chair's button-hide backing and grooved scroll work on the legs told her it was from the Meloric Age.

Kyler dropped her bags on the bed. She began to unpack, then noticed that the room had a window. A dusty blue curtain covered a niche with a sill and a weathered pane that was crisscrossed with wires. She gently lifted it to let the muted light in, tucking it behind its hook. Several similar hooks were affixed to the wall near the bed, for hanging robes and cloaks, she guessed. Fascinated by her surroundings, Kyler nearly forgot that she was in a hurry. She didn't want Leith to be waiting on her again.

The hallway was empty but alive with torchlight. Kyler made her way to the laboratory beyond her cell. Stepping through the doorway, an enormous room opened up before her. Her lips parted in awe, and her eyes danced over spell books, relics, bottles, and charms. The ceiling was high and decorated with a complete dragon skeleton, which hung from gossamer wires and seemed to float above her. The wall-sized window let in a portion of what little light the woods offered.

She drifted over to one of the shelves, scanning the different volumes. There was a bookend in the shape of a seven-pointed star, and a human skull that bore some strange deformity in the jaw. She searched the titles, recognizing some as highly coveted master spell books. She reached up to grab one.

"Don't touch anything," Leith's rough voice rang out.

Kyler flinched, her hand shrinking back from the shelf. The sorcerer entered the room, a large stack of books cradled in his robed arms. He approached the long table in the center and dropped the stack on it with a loud thud. He eyed her suspiciously, then placed one hand on the top book.

"These are yours for the duration," he said. "Each day, you'll read one chapter from each of them."

Kyler moved away from the shelf to examine the books. They were very old, the spines frayed, the covers stained and coarse. Leith turned away to clear off the other table. Kyler watched him as he worked, and in the laboratory's bright lights she was able to study Leith's features. She had expected him to look worn and withered, a sickly thin man with a sharp, severe face. Bound to his books in a dark estate in the middle of a haunted wood, he betrayed her expectations. He looked younger than thirty, she thought, recalling the years of his service to the kingdom. It seemed he had a well-constructed frame under the robes, the smooth fabric draped over strong, broad shoulders, providing an outline of his broad chest.

Kyler blinked and looked away, silently chiding herself and swallowing the lump in her throat. With a few deep breaths, she expelled the sudden heat that had come over her when the blood had rushed to her limbs and face.

"Where did the dragon come from?" she asked him.

"Slain by a Melori warrior and given as a gift to the astronomers for predicting its attack on their city," he answered coldly. "Shall we begin, or have you any other inquiries I can satisfy?"

Kyler was tempted to say that she did, indeed, but thought better of it. "No, Master," she replied, as she tucked a long lock of brown hair behind her ear.

"Very well," he said. "Show me your lighting spell."

"What?" Kyler returned.

"Your lighting spell," he repeated.

"Oh," she said, then held her hand out in front of her. She shaped it like a cup and spoke. "Manus Ignatus."

A detached flame sparked in her palm, small as what a candle would produce. Leith raised a disdainful black eyebrow as he looked at it.

"A long-winded spell for such an insufficient result," he remarked, then blew it out. "Again."

"Manus Ignatus," Kyler repeated, the little flame appearing once more.

Leith muttered with disapproval, then closed her hand over the flame with his own. "Think of your dearest friend," he said.

"I beg your pardon," Kyler replied, the heat coming to her as his fingers gripped her closed fist.

"Magic is your closest companion," he explained impatiently. "It knows your darkest secrets, it feels what you feel, it moves with you. Think of your dearest friend," he repeated. Kyler thought of Rowan, the look on his face when she refused his offer of marriage. Her eyes dropped to the floor. "Look at me," Leith snapped. She obeyed. "Tell me a name."

"Rowan," Kyler answered.

"Do you greet him with a formal title?" he asked.

"No," she said.

"Why not?"

"Our relationship is not formal," she replied.

"Neither is your relationship with your magic. There is no need for formality, no cause to keep to ceremony. Call your magic to you as you would a close companion. Use a simple spell. Again," Leith said.

Kyler paused, recalling how Leith had used 'orb' for his lighting spell. She understood. Leith took his hand from hers and she opened her palm. She cleared her throat.

"Flame," she said strictly. Nothing happened. Her eyes flicked up at her master. He was waiting, his arms crossed over his chest. She looked back down at her palm. "Flame," she said again.

Once more, her hand was empty. Leith heaved a burdened sigh and shifted his weight. "It will not answer to doubt," he stated. "Mean what you say, girl," he told her.

"My name is Kyler," she returned boldly.

"Call your magic, Kyler."

Kyler looked back at her palm. She fixed her gaze on the space, where she longed to call a hundred spells she'd seen the others relish. She stared at her own fingers, still spotted black with ink from a dozen quills that scribbled histories she wished she'd lived. This was her second chance. Perhaps her last one.

"Flame," said Kyler, with a mix of force and gentleness.

A tiny flit of fire appeared in her hand and immediately snuffed out. She stared at her hand as if it had betrayed her. Leith stared blankly at the walls.

"Again," he ordered.

She hesitated. Leith's hand snaked out to grasp her wrist. She flinched.

"You are the master of your magic. Treat it that way!" he said, showing her the palm of her own hand. "Again."

Kyler took a breath. Her entire life flashed before her: all her failures, her sense of self-worth, her own mother having left her to the mercies of the Academy. She suddenly felt anger, a quiet rage at being seen as nothing but a dutiful scribe whose life consisted only of ink and parchment. She closed her eyes.

"Flame," came her voice; it was even, serious, and stern. Behind her closed lids there was a bright light. She opened her eyes to a larger, more robust fire that sprang from her palm and rose high into the air. Leith took a step backward in alarm, but did not counter the spell. Kyler cried out, winced at its brightness, and turned her gaze away. She moved it out farther away from her and shielded her face with her other hand. It slowly settled, and she finally looked at it. She smiled to herself and huffed.

"I don't believe it," she muttered.

"That must be remedied," Leith replied.

He raised one fist toward the unlit sconces, then flicked it open, his fingers spread out. One by one, each torch ignited in sequence. The dragon in the rafters glowed with firelight.

"Let's continue," he said.

The violet light of evening had fallen over the woods. A delicate snowfall could be seen from the windows, stark white flakes gently caressing the black trees. The old witch leaned on her gnarled cane, sipping a glass of wine. Leith appeared behind her following a loud pop, and patted the dust from his collar. The old woman turned away from the window.

"What news of her?" she squeaked.

Leith walked over to a simmering potion, the container and

its liquid suspended upside down in midair over a green flame. He checked it intently, watching bubbles ease through a thick brown liquid. Instead of rising up, the bubbles dropped down, popping as they reached the bottom.

"This will be a long winter," Leith finally answered bitterly. "Wickham knew what he was doing. Her magic is lamentable. She is a scribe, Marisele," he told the old witch with a cynical laugh. "They sent me a scribe as a student."

"She has confused my senses," the old woman confessed angrily, setting the goblet down on her desk, which was cluttered with scattered runes and stones. "I cannot discern whether her presence is helpful or harmful to us. The spirits of the forest seem to like her," she said, squinting her only eye in suspicion.

"She is vibrant," Leith admitted. "And strong. And undaunted by my demands thus far. Of course they like her; she is the only pure thing they've felt in this forest in centuries. Tell me what you see," he said, his eyes glowing blue as he stepped into a shadow.

"The girl knows nothing of Wickham's intentions," the witch said, limping over to a small silver basin filled with water. She waved one wrinkled hand over its still surface. "Her heart is clean. She is trusting," Marisele added with a wicked hiss. "But not a fool."

The water gave way to ripples, and images flashed in the waves.

Leith joined her at the basin, watching as the young girl's figure appeared as a distorted, shifting silhouette, as if he were viewing her through a sheer gray fabric that was blowing in the wind. She was seated at the desk in her cell, laboring over her books, knees drawn up to her chest. She turned a page.

"Will she be a problem for us?" Leith asked dryly.

"She could be useful—if you teach her useful spells," Marisele answered. "My lord, what happened to you?" the witch inquired with a sudden change of tone, having noticed a small, bleeding pelt mark on his neck.

"A lesson gone wrong," he grumbled. "My new pupil had severe difficulty with a simple transport spell."

Marisele returned her gaze to the rippling water. Kyler was now pacing her cell with a book in one hand and biting the fingernails of the other. "She wishes to please you," the old woman observed.

"Under any other circumstances, I would surely welcome it," Leith replied, taking a seat. "But, I can't have dramatics when we are so close to our end. The potion is nearly ready, and I've finally reached the heart of Lamentiose."

"I mean she wishes to earn your approval. She admires you. This you can use to your advantage," the witch remarked, then coughed.

"You will join us for dinner tonight," Leith ordered, looking out the window at the diminishing sunlight. "There is something I need you to do."

Marisele's eye blinked.

"But, I don't . . . My lord, I don't think that . . ."

"I think you and I should get to know this Kyler more intimately," Leith interrupted. "Let's turn over some rocks," he said, then sneered to himself.

CHAPTER THREE
THE LIBRARY

Kyler closed her book and looked out the window at the purple light, which was growing darker by the minute. Her gaze ambled up to the dusty chandelier. She placed the book on the desk with the rest of the stack and stepped underneath the chandelier. Holding out her hand, she shut one eye and turned her head away.

"Flame," she said.

A tiny flare appeared, then immediately burned out in her palm. Kyler cleared her throat. She looked up once more at the lamp, doing her best to aim it just right. She held her hand far out in front, and turned her face from it.

"Flame!" she repeated with more fervor.

Instantly, a blazing fire leapt from her palm towards the ceiling. Kyler shrieked and quickly jumped back, wringing her fingers as smoke seeped from them. She looked down at her hand. It was stained with soot marks, but otherwise undamaged. Kyler then noticed that the room was glowing with firelight. She glanced up at the chandelier. The lamp's six candles were lit, and tiny embers flaked downward where the cobwebs had been consumed.

"Ha!" she blurted with delight, then followed with a gasp of sudden realization at the growing shadows of the room. "Sunset!" she said aloud, and dashed across the hall. The privy was small, damp, and cold, containing just a wash basin, a bench with a hole, and a bathtub, all affixed to a large wooden cistern that hung above her head. She'd seen such a device before in Storm Side—a tank that collected rainwater and distributed it via a series of pipes. There was a lever near the basin, attached to a crude metal spout. She tugged on it, and as the water flowed out, she was able to wash her face and hands.

Kyler dried her hands quickly and rushed toward the spiral staircase. She was greeted by a warm light from the main room's great fireplace, which bathed the hanging murals and antique furniture in a pleasant golden luster. The space was quiet and empty, but an appealing aroma was coming from the lit archway to the left. She walked under the arch and entered a dining hall, with a long wooden table stretched down the center and a tall, ornate cabinet with chipped dishes behind clouded glass doors. A feeble chandelier hung over the table. There were three place settings at the far end.

Suddenly, she felt something nudge her, and a short, shrill scream pierced the quiet hall.

Kyler whipped around, a strange sound of fright escaping her lips. She leapt backward from a withering old wretch of a woman, whose long, wispy white hair draped over her hunched shoulders. She was glaring at Kyler with one lecherous brown eye. Kyler caught her breath, waiting for the woman to speak, but she only stood there, leaning on a gnarled wooden cane and looking like a cloud of poisonous gas.

Kyler swallowed. "How do you do?" she asked bravely.

Nothing. The eye searched her, looking her over carefully, suspiciously. There were footsteps, then a tall shadow arrived.

"Say hello, Marisele," Leith intoned. He carried a large steaming bowl. "Marisele is my colleague. We both prefer a life of solitude."

Leith's faintly glowing eyes shifted, as if reprimanding the old woman and urging her to cooperate. Marisele finally reached out a stiff, wrinkled hand tipped with blackened fingernails. Kyler complied, giving her own hand and squeezing lightly. Without warning, the old woman had yanked on it, pulling Kyler closer and forcing her down a foot to meet her gaze. Kyler yelped, startled, but obliged Marisele by allowing her a better look. She waited as the woman inspected her, the scrutinizing brown eye roaming over her face.

"How do you do?" the old woman finally squawked with sarcasm.

Kyler did her best not to react to the odor that came from behind the set of rotting teeth. It was a foul mixture, like stale wine and decaying flesh.

"Shall we?" Leith prompted stoically, advancing toward the table.

Marisele released Kyler and followed him. Kyler stood up straight, and thought she heard the old woman chuckle to herself as she took a seat. Leith began ladling a dark purple soup into the three smaller bowls on the table. Kyler joined them at the only remaining empty chair. Leith sat at the end. Kyler and Marisele sat across from each other. There was a moment of silence as her master and his associate began to eat. At one point, Leith stretched his neck to take a spoonful, grunted, and placed a hand on the back of his neck. Kyler lowered her spoon.

"Master," she said. "I just wanted to tell you again how sorry I am . . ."

"No need," Leith interrupted between spoonfuls. "As you said, you haven't studied for many years. Accidents are inevitable. Tell me, Kyler," he said, pausing to swallow. "How is it that you became a scribe? What interested you so that you would be inclined to spend your days deep in the bowels of the Chamber of Shadows?"

Kyler looked down at her soup and took up her spoon. "I suppose that was an accident as well, my lord," she began. "As you may have already concluded, I am not skilled in the Craft. After many failed attempts at study, I became discouraged and found my solace in the library. I was fascinated particularly by ancient history, and asked the headmistress if I could modify a rather poorly organized record of the Tawdry Cape Massacre. She agreed," explained Kyler, tucking her hair behind one ear. "I suppose I must have done rather well. The headmistress suggested I discontinue my studies in sorcery and become a full-time scribe instead. Is this plume root?" Kyler asked suddenly, dipping her spoon into the stew.

"Yes," Leith answered. "There aren't many who can place it."

"I've eaten it once on a trip through Black Burrow. I've read that it only grows underground and requires an extraordinary amount of moisture," Kyler said.

Leith and his witch traded a look. He cleared his throat. "We are fortunate," he said, "that the cellar was poorly constructed. The walls were hollowed from the earth, and the snow melts down into the soil. The plume root began to grow to our surprise. Tell me," said Leith, taking a quick sip from his cup, "in your studies of history, you must have come to very educated conclusions about our many wars and rebellions. There are so few students of the Academy who ground their convictions in fact rather than what their masters dictate."

Kyler hesitated. "I suppose so," she answered. "I try to resist judgment, though it becomes difficult sometimes," she said.

"And whom do you judge, my apprentice?" Leith inquired. "What figures of our history do you find most unrighteous?"

"Well," Kyler said. "Malantheus, of course." She heard the old woman make a kind of hissing sound with her throat. "He was a vicious murderer with an arrogant vision," she continued boldly.

"Arrogant," Leith repeated, his long, slender fingers wrapping like a lazy spider around his cup. "Is it arrogant to disagree with the idea that a sorcerer's magic should be regulated by those who are not gifted with it? Is it arrogant to fight for the freedom to use magic at one's own will as he chooses?"

Kyler frowned, feeling affronted. "You defend Malantheus?" she said.

"I present a perspective," Leith corrected. "Surely, a revered scholar such as yourself can explore an alternate viewpoint. Is this arrogance, apprentice?"

Kyler thought carefully. "It is arrogant when one's own will is to subjugate others. Malantheus struck down anyone who opposed him. His tyranny went beyond a man simply longing for freedom."

"And how do you define tyranny? Some would say it was tyranny he was fighting against."

"Only his followers said that. Holding sorcerers accountable for murder and abuse of power isn't tyranny. I read the Treaty. It was a truce."

"Then you didn't read it properly," said Leith, closely trailing her words. "What are the first few lines?"

Kyler paused, staring at him. "The time has come, in light of the many crimes committed by . . . by the corrupt among us, that we hereby . . . hereby . . ."

"Hereby impose sanctions on the use of magic for the purpose of evil, violations of which are punishable by death or worse," Leith finished for her. "The authors of the Treaty make their own definition of 'crimes' and 'evil'. When men are left with the power to make those interpretations, that's tyranny."

"He used his gauntlet to assume ultimate power. He mobilized the Black Trade and used his magic to murder innocent people who opposed him," she said.

"All rebellions cost innocent people," Leith countered. "It just depends on the cause. Malantheus believed that we, as sorcerers, shouldn't be told how to use our magic."

"Malantheus believed he had the right to use his power to control Salyndria. What if every sorcerer felt the same?"

"Then I suppose it would be a fight for who should be able to have that power. That's what wars are about. His was no different."

"Except that he lost," Kyler said indignantly.

Leith stopped for a moment and smirked at her, like someone holding back a secret.

"Your medallion," Marisele squeaked suddenly, and pointed. She squinted in the candlelight as she leaned forward. "How did you come by it?"

Kyler instinctively placed her hand over it, her fingers touching the amber and emeralds set in smooth silver. "It is an heirloom," she answered. "I have ancestors who served the priesthood of Amaleus."

"Yes, Amaleus," Leith repeated with a soft laugh. "The old forgotten god of justice and compassion. It was his priests that fought to save the tortured spirits that roam these very woods."

"They believed Malantheus's disciples deserved a trial," Kyler stated. "But the kingdom refused them mercy."

"And what say you to that?" Leith continued.

"I say those who are guilty deserve punishment."

"So you agree that the Necromantis spell was a just sentence?"

"No!" Kyler exclaimed. "It was a cruel and brutal damnation brought on by hatred and vengeance rather than reason," she told them fiercely. Kyler thought she saw Leith's smooth, handsome lips turn upward slightly. She swallowed and sat back, displeased with herself. "I'm sorry," she confessed in a calmer voice.

"You've suffered ridicule for wearing that bauble, haven't you?" asked Leith, resuming his meal.

"On occasion," Kyler answered quietly.

"You needn't worry about such things here," he replied.

To her surprise, Leith's severe blue eyes seemed to reveal a sudden hint of warmth. It was the first sign of welcome she'd been given since her arrival. It was quiet again, and Kyler ate her plume root stew as nightfall claimed the winter sky outside the windows. Little else was said as the three of them finished dinner, each of them clearing their bowls and spoons. Kyler offered a tepid "good night" and a short bow to each of them. She quickly turned, not waiting for a response. She was relieved to finally make her way up to her quarters.

Closing the door behind her, she leaned against it, staring up at the chandelier. The room was darkening quickly. She still carried the small flame in her palm to lead the way up. Kyler lit the candle on the table and extinguished her light spell. She had dusted the bookcase and placed a few of her volumes there. She was angry with herself that, as a scribe, she had not been able to recite more of the Treaty. Looking around, she realized she was to spend these months with a man who defended Malantheus against the Academy and their punishments. Perhaps she shouldn't have spoken about it, but she felt it was her duty to speak up, even despite his rank. Kyler shed her brown robes, revealing a plain, thin gown underneath. She was worried that her first night would be a sleepless one.

The privy was dimly lit. Kyler had changed into her night clothes—a heavier white gown and a worn pair of white slippers. Over this she wore a warm gray bed robe, and her curtain of brown hair was tied back with a chord. She pushed back the lever to close off the water before stepping out. She lingered for a moment in the hallway, staring into the shadowed laboratory with a sense of wonder. She drifted closer.

Beyond the doorway, jars and bottles reflected the stream of moonlight that crept in through the crack in the drapes. Kyler crossed the room and pulled them back with one strong motion, and a loud sweeping sound followed. The moonlight poured in, saturating everything in chalky white. The dragon skeleton looked even more menacing as the light touched it, its bones almost glowing. Kyler found herself smiling up at it, marveling at its villainous skull and hollowed eyes. Just then, there was movement.

Kyler moved quickly into the shadows. In the narrow hall was the figure of a young man about her age with his head bowed. He wore a tattered purple robe, the color of the Order of Spirit, and his skin was withered and pallid. His hair was wet and strung with weeds as if he'd come up from a lake.

She swallowed and moved toward the hall. Kyler reached the doorway, slowly stepped into the light and exhaled quietly. Suddenly, the figure moved. Her heart beat wildly as she watched him turn and trudge down the hall, keeping his head bowed. She had seen a ghost before, having spent time in the Chamber of Spirit, where they specialized in conjuring them. She knew how they behaved, and that when they appeared without provocation, it was because they wanted to communicate. She could only assume that in this cursed place, this figure was not of the living. When he reached the stairway, he stopped. Kyler took another few steps closer. The ghost vanished into the shadowy stairway, his torn purple robe trailing him. Kyler held out her hand, palm up.

"Flame," she commanded. To her surprise, the magic obeyed, and a small fire sprouted from her hand. "Hmm," she huffed, bewildered.

Kyler rushed after the spirit, holding her light out in front of her as she descended the spiral staircase. Once she reached the bottom, she spotted him as he walked through the archway leading to the library. The fireplace housed only a pile of embers, and Kyler looked cautiously around at the main room using what light her spell offered. There was no one. She skipped once, trying to keep up with the ghost as she headed down a short hall. A heavy oak door was at the end, standing ajar.

She slowly pushed it open all the way, bringing her light in with her. Kyler's lips parted in awe as her flame suddenly grew larger, illuminating a large rectangular room, the walls made up of misshapen sepia-colored boulders and dotted with more unlit sconces. She recognized the stones as Cognitite, a smooth, dark red mineral believed by the ancients to inspire deep thought. Jutting out from the walls on either side were tall shelves that formed a wide aisle. They were made of thick, blemished mahogany and marked on the ends by carved symbols. Kyler looked to the lantern hanging near the door and lit it with her flame.

She closed her hand and took up the lantern, searching the room for the specter. The shelves, which were packed with antique books, reached toward an arched ceiling made up of panels that depicted old gods, goddesses, and starry skies. Kyler marveled at how orderly the volumes were kept, stacked in accordance with the ancient alphabet— more for tradition than practicality, she imagined. At the end of the aisle, there was a moderate-sized window with Nythos's seven-pointed star at its center in colored glass. The snow spun beyond the pane, its white flakes bright against the dark night. The room opened up like a T: a work desk and cabinets in the corner to her left, and a made bed with a canopy on her right.

Kyler frowned at the bed. It was flush against the dark red stone wall, the curtain drawn back. Her expression changed. *For late night studies,* she guessed, running her hand over the dented wood frame. A sound made her turn suddenly. There was shuffling, like someone taking a book from a shelf. Kyler stepped back to the aisle and listened. She took a few more steps, looking right and left between the shelves. Holding up her lantern to read a few of the titles, she noticed a golden plaque bolted to the shelf end that noted the date of the last Regium Comet. The last time it passed over the observatory was more than three hundred years ago.

Kyler flinched as an image flashed in the smooth gold. It was the spirit in the purple robe, his head erect and staring with crimson eyes from the shelf behind her. The eyes were rimmed as if with soot, and his cheeks were sunken in a colorless face.

Kyler whirled. Her limbs tingled and her spine seized her. The lantern light revealed nothing but the empty aisle and the unoccupied shelf behind her. He had vanished.

She exhaled with relief and ventured cautiously over to where the ghost had appeared. The volumes placed there were organized differently. Not only were they arranged by the new alphabet, but they seemed to be newer than the rest, and all related to the rise and fall of Malantheus. Kyler's hazel eyes squinted at the wearing print on the spines: *History of the Necromantis Spell, Rise of the Black Trade, Dangers of the Abuse of Magic.*

Kyler continued to scan the titles, already planning a return visit to the library, when she would have more time. After dinner would be perfect, she thought. It seemed neither her master nor his one-eyed associate used the room at night. Suddenly, she heard a short sweeping sound only inches away. She looked up, expecting to see the blood-red eyes staring back at her. There was nothing, except one volume protruding from the rest, a black, leather-bound book shining in the lantern light.

Kyler reached out for it. *A History of the Nefarious Gauntlet,* read the faded letters. She looked around warily, clutched the book to her chest and returned to the desk, where she set down the lantern. She settled herself near the window where the snow danced outside. She opened the book and began to read.

Kyler knew some of the details of the gauntlet's creation, but she was surprised to find conflicting accounts of its appearance. There was a sketch of it in the book, a regular-looking soldier's glove with chain mail and metalwork surrounding it. She turned the pages, reading through witness accounts of the battles. Some reported that the knuckles had sharp spikes, while others described it as smooth bronze and metal with no spikes. She guessed that some details were probably exaggerated.

The next few chapters told of the gauntlet's powers, forged by the Kingdom's blacksmiths who had defected to join the Black Trade, which explained the soldier's design. The metal itself was enchanted by Black Trade sorcerers with forbidden spells from the Grimoire at the point of melting, then poured into a mold stolen from the kingdom's armories. The spells allowed the wearer to bond with the object, understanding its master's will.

"The most notorious spell that completed its creation was the *dominion* spell," Kyler whispered aloud as she read. "Giving the wearer complete control over any soul he desires, living or dead." She turned a page. "The details of how the gauntlet bonds with its wearer are still unclear." Kyler knew the Black Trade did its best to hide or destroy all of its secrets.

She leaned back against the wall and looked out the window. There was no sign of the apparition. She couldn't tell how long she'd been reading. She put the book back in its proper place and left the library to return to her room, hoping to get enough rest for her lesson the next day.

Leith waited. He surveyed his apprentice carefully and cleared his throat. Kyler quickened her pace. She prepared a potion on the long table in the laboratory, a cluster of jars and bottles in front of her. She was nearly finished, dropping a handful of aster flowers, dried and crushed, into the small caldron and lighting the burner beneath it. She smacked her hands together to rid them of the excess and stood back from the table.

"Done," she announced.

Leith approached the table and examined the potion. He traced the rim of the caldron and peered down at the bubbling liquid. "Very good," he said. His eyes flicked up at her. "Now, drink it."

"Drink it?" Kyler replied nervously.

"Must you repeat everything I say?" Leith asked coldly. "Take the ladle and drink it."

Kyler hesitated, then took up the ladle lying next to the caldron. She regarded her surroundings as she dunked it into the potion. Leith surmised she was taking inventory of the room's metal objects. She sipped it with great apprehension, and squeezed her eyes shut at the taste and smell, a strong, musky, wilted flower flavor, if he remembered correctly. She lowered the long spoon from her mouth, the potion leaving a glisten on her lips. Leith found himself staring and immediately averted his gaze. Kyler tensed, her hand clutching the spoon, waiting. After a moment, a look of stark disappointment gripped the amiable features, and her hand gradually relaxed.

"I'm sorry, my lord," she confessed, letting the ladle drop onto the table.

Leith, however, was still alert. As much as he disliked her intrusion and abhorred being disturbed, he had developed faith in his new apprentice's ability to learn. She was unskilled, yes, but her discipline was impeccable, a quality he had not had the luxury of in even the finest of his students. Suddenly, the ladle trembled, and Kyler jumped as it abruptly leapt from the table and clung to her arm. A warm smile stretched across her lips, so blithe and infectious that it almost prompted Leith to mimic it.

"Ha, ha!" she exclaimed excitedly, reaching out her arm and moving it slowly up and down. It was stuck to her brown robes, fastening the green stripe on her sleeve to her arm underneath it. "I did it!" But then an unseen force launched her forward, and she stumbled into the table with a cry of pain.

A small iron bookend had flown from the nearby shelf and attached itself to her shoulder. Leith was smirking now, but soon grew concerned when more objects began to seek her out. Kyler quickly shielded herself with her arms as additional trinkets came at her. A bronze compass and ink well were pulled from the writing desk across the room, the well spilling on the floor as it traveled and splashing a black stain on Kyler's robes.

The wires holding up the dragon began to shift and stretch, and an iron rack holding powder jars moved toward her, but it was blocked by the table. The sorcerer's hands were suddenly pulled outward by his many silver rings, which slipped from his fingers and struck Kyler's forearms.

"Master!" she cried out desperately, now fully decorated with metal objects.

"Abscido!" Leith commanded loudly.

There was a dissonant commotion as the sound of a dozen metal trinkets and instruments hit the floor at once. Kyler was still shielding herself, small bleeding abrasions visible on her arms. Leith rushed around the table, stepping over what had fallen. He reached out, took her arms, and slowly lowered them from her face. Kyler glanced around at the disorder, her bright green eyes swelled with chagrin.

"I'm so sorry," she said again.

"It's no fault of yours," Leith stated, inspecting the cuts on her arms. "The measurements of the ingredients have never produced this powerful a result," he said, frowning. "I must have miscalculated," he added, displeased to admit a possible mistake.

He turned to the table and reached for a wooden case, which he opened to reveal several clean strips of cloth and a small bottle filled with clear liquid. Tearing one in half, he took up the bottle and dampened the cloth with it.

"Where did those come from?" Kyler asked.

"I keep them handy," Leith muttered, and gingerly applied the cloth to the wounds on her arm.

Kyler froze, bracing herself for a sting, but it didn't come. She kept still for him, waiting patiently as he cleaned the abrasions, holding her arm up by the elbow with one hand.

"What is that stuff?" she asked him.

"A remedy made from peppermint and foster flower," Leith answered. "Its healing properties are praised by the Chamber of Light." His eyes shifted from his task to her face. She was watching him work, then met his gaze. "It doesn't hurt," he said softly.

He had stopped his hands except for his right thumb, which was languidly stroking her wrist as he looked at her.

"It doesn't," Kyler agreed in a halting whisper.

Leith blinked, stepped back and placed the stopper back on the bottle. "We're finished for today," he announced, packing away the wooden case.

Kyler pulled down her sleeves and looked around. "But, I should help you tidy up," she offered, picking up the bookend and placing it on the table. "Master, your rings," she said, scooping up the lot of them.

"Thank you," he answered, quickly taking his silver rings from her cupped hands. "But you may go. I'll see to this," he said, waving a hand at the disrupted laboratory.

"Please, let me at least . . ."

"You may go," he repeated curtly.

Kyler hesitated. She finally left the room, pausing to take one puzzled look back before vanishing through the doorway and into the hall. Leith slipped the rings back onto his fingers and reached out his hand, fingers spread, toward the iron rack.

"Impelium," he said.

The rack slid backward and settled in its original home. Leith picked up the other objects that had stuck to Kyler and set them on the table. There was the ink stain on the floor, but he decided to let it dry. It was not the only thing that had been spilled in the last few days, and he had given up on keeping the floor spot-free. With one last look around, he left the laboratory.

Leith materialized and quickly crossed his study to grab the carafe of wine. He could feel Marisele's eye on him. He had noticed that there was an aroma about his apprentice, a light perfume he couldn't quite place that abruptly left him whenever he exited the room she occupied. What usually replaced it was the scent of damp decay, the musty odor of old books. He poured himself a glass and immediately took a hearty swallow.

"How long before your Intrinsic Potion is finished?" Leith barked over his shoulder.

"Not long, but you must be patient. The more the subject has hidden, the longer it takes," the witch explained. "Consider yourself lucky. The girl is an open book, but . . ."

"But what?" Leith growled.

"The potion is designed to reveal one's innermost secrets, some things they might not even know about themselves. Something is taking longer than I anticipated. When we have our look into her mind, we'll see how easy it will be to turn her," Marisele squeaked as she peered into the glass jar where the ingredients were fermenting, including one of Kyler's long brown hairs.

Leith had her take it from the girl just before their first dinner, instructing the old woman to startle her as a distraction. She turned the jar around in her hands. It was half full of a dark green paste with flecks of yellow. Leith took another long swallow from his cup.

"I should get down to the passageway," he reminded himself. "The more I can strip from the rocks, the better," he said, then paused. "I can hear them now," he added gravely, staring off at the cold, dark stone walls of his study. "They make the most unsettling sounds."

"You're close to the surface!" Marisele wheezed, then coughed. "The Hypnogoths haven't detected you, but take care. They shriek when nightfall comes. It is their way of welcoming it. They are older than magic, and that means yours won't work against them. You know how violently they protect their treasures, and they will not be pleased to find the most coveted of their collection stolen."

"Of course," Leith replied sourly, gulping down the remaining wine. "Keep me updated," he said, grabbing up a cluster of tools in a leather pouch before exiting.

CHAPTER FOUR

THE DISCOVERY

The winter grew colder as the days passed, but the observatory stayed warm. Leith mentioned that he'd enchanted each torch to generate the heat of four, and any time Kyler was especially chilly, she would sit in the main room near the fireplace with her study books. Dinner was her least favorite part of the day, as she always felt watched by Marisele's leery eye over plume root stew and a ration of whitefish from the traps near the coast. Kyler also believed the spirits were toying with her. She had not yet seen another specter, but items in her cell would be moved and arranged in a strange way whenever she returned from the laboratory.

The library, once again, had become her only place of solace, and she spent most nights studying Malantheus's sordid history. Kyler had become fascinated by it, trying to imagine what the Necromantis curse would be like. She'd first read about it in her second year at the Chamber of Shadow. It was a restricted spell used only for the foulest of murderers, designed to torment them with the same agony they caused their victims for all eternity. Execution was never necessary—the criminal would waste away in his own madness, starving to death or committing suicide. But the curse continued even after that, the tortured spirit forced to linger in the darkness of his own bloody transgressions forever.

What befell Malantheus's followers was different. After he was defeated and the whereabouts of his legion came to light, the Academy devised a newer, crueler derivative of the spell. The headmasters used his gauntlet, originally enchanted to communicate with and command his disciples, to deflect the anguish of all of Malantheus' victims onto them, in addition to their own. The effect was unprecedented. Solemn

Woods became the resting place of more than four hundred tormented lunatics, driven to kill themselves and each other only to roam the afterlife in eternal affliction.

Kyler often slammed the books shut suddenly as if to close in an evil spirit. She would replace them on the shelf and step back as if never wishing to touch them again. But, each night after dinner, she found herself returning to learn more.

Her lessons had become less embarrassing, and she'd managed to govern basic spells under the tutelage of her exacting master. Leith was strict, impatient, and often unorthodox, teaching her more complicated spells before the essential ones. But, it seemed to work to her benefit.

Despite occasional mishaps, Kyler was finally becoming a sorceress.

"Again," said Leith sharply, reaching out to snatch the bookend from the air. He had developed a type of defense during Kyler's lessons, ready with a suspension spell once the object became unruly. He had also refrained from choosing items liable to break into pieces, such as glass jars. "Concentrate," he ordered, dropping the bookend down on the table in front of her.

Kyler pushed up her brown sleeves and placed her hand over the object, fingers stiff, palm straight. "Levitum Momentus," she repeated.

The bookend trembled, slowly lifted from the table, and abruptly launched across the room toward the window. Leith quickly raised his ringed fingers.

"Stop," he commanded.

The bookend froze, catching the light of late afternoon through the small opening in the curtain. Leith marched over to it, retrieving it again. He made his way back to the table and set the bookend before her.

"It is too advanced a spell for me, my lord," she declared, raising her head and straightening her posture.

"You are bold," he replied dryly, "to believe you can decide that for yourself."

He came around to stand behind her, reached around for her hand and placed it over the bookend. He felt her stiffen as he drew close, the soft brown hair brushing his cheek as he looked over her shoulder. "Not like that," he snapped, as she straightened out her fingers. He jerked her hand as if to shake something from it. "Relax your fingers. Let them float as if in water, languid, gentle," he told her, fitting his long fingers over hers. "Magic moves through your senses. It lends itself to your will, it is not tyrannized by it."

Her hand was dwarfed by his. He guided it down over the object and slowly drew his away. "Close your eyes," he said in her ear. Her long lashes dropped, and her head lifted slightly. "Say the spell," he told her, taking a step back.

Kyler's hand hovered loosely over the bookend, her fingers shaped like a drooping claw. She breathed in deeply and exhaled.

"Levitum Momentus," she said sharply.

The bookend lifted from the table and hung in midair just under Kyler's hand. Her eyes were open now, wide with excitement and staring at the object she'd managed to control.

"Now put it somewhere," Leith said.

Kyler straightened her shoulders. With great care, she moved her hand. The bookend followed. She turned toward the bookshelf to her right, and slowly undulated her fingers to push the object forward. It obeyed, gliding mildly toward its intended destination. It sailed to the top shelf, high near the ceiling where the dragon's tailbone hung. Kyler smiled with pride, then abruptly frowned, her eyes popping open wide. She ducked. Leith glanced up in time to avoid the bookend's angry and violent return as it swooped down over the table and back up toward the roof.

There was the echoing sound of wires being struck and disturbed, and Leith tracked the flying object as it flitted about the room. The dragon's immense skeleton swayed. Kyler was inert. He had taught her not to move whenever he was forced to remedy a spell gone awry. She was braced for the object to fly toward her, but Leith was finally able to halt its course.

"Stop!" he commanded, arresting it on its way toward a cluster of beakers.

It happened in a matter of seconds. In one instant, his eyes were on the bookend, ready to summon it back. The next, the alarming sound of a wire snapping filled the laboratory, and the dragon's massive skull, with its sharp, deadly teeth exposed, dropped and swung at a great speed toward his apprentice. It fell from the ceiling on the pendulum of its own wire, soaring downward at her head as if its bloodthirsty will still lived in its bones. Just as Leith opened his mouth with a spell to rescue her, the dragon's skull had been destroyed.

There was a tumultuous bang, a fireless explosion. Kyler's slender robed figure could be seen through the cloud of ashen dust. She had shielded herself with her arm, and as she cautiously lowered it, the bewildered look in her eyes was revealed. The skull was obliterated inches from her face, almost as if hit by a force field around her. It had burst into a puff of debris so close to its destination that Kyler's robe and hair were coated in white powder. Now she covered her mouth with her hand, staring down at what broken pieces remained of the creature's notoriously indestructible components. There was a small pile on the floor, fragments of the jawbone still visible. Kyler's hand shifted from her mouth to her chest.

"Thank you, master," she panted with gratitude and relief.

Leith's black eyebrows drew sternly together. What had Wickham done to him? She was manipulating him! This scribe who knew no magic suddenly capable of such a spell? He wouldn't be fooled. He motioned for the bookend as if it were a servant he was calling over. It glided right into his hand, and he clenched it tightly as he marched over.

"I've done nothing!" he thundered, tossing the bookend on the table, the heavy bronze landing so loudly it made Kyler jump. He continued toward her. "How did you accomplish this?" he demanded, rushing up on her, searching her expression.

Kyler took a step back. "I . . . I don't know, my lord," she said.

"Don't lie to me!" Leith shot back, stepping forward and gripping her at the shoulders. "Tell me how it was done!"

"I didn't do this, master!" she answered back. "I couldn't have! Please, let me go."

"You're a fool to think you can trick me, girl. No apprentice is capable of such a spell, let alone a scribe. You'll tell me or I'll throw you to the woods, do you hear me? I'll let the spirits have you!" he roared with his eyes fixed on her, his long fingers forming a vise around each of her arms.

"Let her go!" another voice echoed.

Leith turned. Marisele leaned on her cane in the laboratory doorway. "You know she tells the truth, my lord. Let her go."

He looked back at the girl. She looked frightened and confused, her hair specked with powder and her startled eyes pleading up at him.

There was no shadow; only the evening light from the window and the torches crossed her beautiful face. Leith released her. She immediately stepped back from him and glanced warily over at Marisele.

"Go," he told her quietly, staring at the pile of dust on the floor.

This time, Kyler didn't protest. She made her way around the table and avoided Marisele as she passed quickly through the doorway and into the hall. Leith and his aged associate remained. The old witch limped into the room, her one eye gazing up at the now headless skeleton poised in the ceiling.

"You'd better come up to the study," she advised.

Kyler swung the two doors that led out from a second-floor corridor wide open and stepped out into the cold evening air. She gripped the stone rail in front of her and stared down at the weed-scattered yard below. The sun retreated behind the ominous black trees, leaving a lavender glimmer in the overcast sky. She noticed the white dust on her sleeves and hurriedly began to brush it away as if it were toxic. She tousled her hair, too, ridding it of the ancient remains of one of Salyndria's deadliest monsters.

With a few more shakes and brushes, she finally settled, trembling as she gazed out over the obscure landscape. The spire of the Chamber of Sight was visible from the second floor over the crippled black branches. Kyler's mind spun, trying to piece together what had happened. She remembered seeing the skull swing loose, turning her head as it soared toward her, and wishing very hard that something would stop it. The tips of her fingers tingled just before it exploded. But—she couldn't have! She didn't even say the words. An apprentice at her level could be severely punished for such a destructive incantation.

Leith's glowing blue eyes came back to her, searching her face, peering down at her as if he were trying to steal her soul away. Kyler felt a chill. She remembered reading about a restricted spell used for interrogating violators of magical misuse. It marks the eyes with a passing shadow when the subject tells a lie. Perhaps Master Leith uses such a spell whenever he pleases. She stared out at the vanishing sun and the snow-spotted trees, whose black fingers reached over the courtyard.

She wondered if she really had performed a spell beyond her stripes. It was the first time she'd seen her instructor so confounded. Amidst the confusion, frustration, and shame, Kyler found herself smiling.

The door flew open and Leith stepped in. He held it open for Marisele, who hobbled up the last step and entered the study.

"I certainly hope you can explain this," he told her as he shut the door.

"Patience," she answered back, and crossed the cluttered room toward her table. "You'll be pleased, I think," she said.

The table was laden with feathers and severed beaks, bottles that held claws and tiny eyeballs from different animals. They had all been pushed aside to make room for a large, rectangular wooden tray with carvings all around it. The jar that held the potion was empty but for a pasty green residue; the potion itself had been poured into the tray. Leith joined her at the table as she leaned over it. The liquid had made a shapeless design in the wood, and Marisele looked down at it as if reading a book.

"Tell me," Leith persisted.

"Your pretty little apprentice has much more power than we thought," Marisele began. "Her magic is in its rawest form, summoned when its user is threatened—a survival instinct. I have seen it before. Such magic cannot be trained by petty levitation spells; it must be called by a more pertinent need. That's why her previous masters failed her—they were trying to light a candle with a wildfire."

Leith paused. "You're saying she botches her spells and breaks my instruments because she has more power than she can control?" he asked in a hoarse laugh. "Perhaps your skills are defective in your very old age, my friend."

"You know it to be true," Marisele countered severely. "She had no idea where her own power came from, you saw it. Only the most accomplished sorcerers can brandish a spell that even pierces a dragon's hide, let alone turns its bones to dust. The girl is a rare find, my lord. Wickham is a blind fool to send her to us."

"And how am I to train her, now?" Leith said, throwing off his long black robe and hanging it on a hook. "I suppose I could throw knives at her and wait for the magic to reveal itself," he continued cynically. He reached for a long-sleeved linen shirt and pulled it on. "Or let the spirits of the woods drive her mad with visions of their murders and wait for her power to save her."

"There are ways," Marisele told him, raising a wrinkled finger. "You are the clever one, aren't you, Leith? You found their passageway, did you not? You found Malantheus' resting place. An army of ghosts waits patiently for you to call them to arms, to seek their revenge on the Academy. It is you who will bring new order to Salyndria and give magic the freedom it deserves after you take the throne. Surely, you can wield your clumsy young pupil. Unless . . ."

Marisele paused, a hiss coming from her throat. "You are reluctant to harm her."

Leith's luminescent blue eyes narrowed. "You forget who saved you from your prison, old woman. You forget who will keep silent about your cowardice when your fellows are awakened. Imagine what they would do to you if they recognized their colleague, still alive after all this time," he said. "You should worry about your own conscience, not mine. Tell me what else you see."

Marisele looked back at the wooden tray. She took it by the handles on either side and tilted it backwards and forward, making the liquid run. "She is strong-willed, and her dedication to the Academy is steadfast. She is pure, as we suspected. But . . ." She paused, reading the liquid.

"But, what?" Leith prompted impatiently.

"There is a man. He is in her heart, but she does not love him. The only love she keeps hides in memories of her mother. There is abandonment, alienation. This is the source of her greatest fears and doubts. She has questions," hissed Marisele with delight. "She longs to prove herself worthy. There is wildness beneath her innocence, a dark streak," the old witch said, looking closely at the tray. "They were right to place her in the Chamber of Shadows. I see her dreams—they are of adventure. Your apprentice is not as content pouring over her archives as she would have us all think."

"I didn't need your odious potion to see that," Leith snapped. He crossed the room to the beaker that was suspended upside down over a flame. "I can use her weaknesses, but she doesn't yet trust me fully. If she truly longs for adventure, she shall have it. I can make her part of the history she studies."

Leith gazed into the boiling potion. "It will be too tempting an offer to refuse."

There was a torch burning on the wall. A man and woman writhed on the bed. His skin reflected the firelight, and his black hair shined like oil. Kyler's slender legs wrapped his waist, and the sound of her blissful moaning echoed off the cold stone walls. His lips covered hers in a long kiss. The medallion shined against her bare skin, her white gown fallen and draped around her middle. She yielded beneath his powerful frame.

Her eyes were closed in rapture, her head turned to one side as he murmured softly in her ear with a deep, gravelly voice. The sorcerer's eyes were unlit, lacking the magical glow that was so legendary. His back was slick with sweat, and his shoulders quaked with each thrust. Kyler's beautiful, sinuous form writhed in his arms, her neck rising up for another kiss. He answered it with his tongue, plunging it into her mouth gingerly again and again as he rocked his groin into hers, matching the rhythm. He groaned against her lips, his thrusts becoming faster and more forceful.

"Leith," came her bell-like voice in a weak whisper.

Rowan's eyes flew open. Sweating and angry, he threw off the covers, his brown hair hanging in tangles about his shoulders. He sat at the edge of his bed, looking around at his cell, trying to rid himself of the dream. Finally, he stood and crossed the cell to his basin. He splashed his face with water, but the images still plagued him: the flashes of Master Leith's spindly fingers sliding up her thighs, his mouth on her breasts. The young man pulled on his red robe and smoothed down his hair. Throwing open his cell door, he marched down the long, torch-lined corridor toward Headmaster Wickham's chamber.

"I'll send you to the dungeons, so help me," the old man bellowed as an assistant ushered Rowan into the study. "This had better be important."

Headmaster Wickham was dressed in his night robe and cap. His mottled hands lay palm-side down on his desk as he leaned forward, waiting to hear what urgent news warranted his waking. The old man's gossamer beard was in a long, frazzled braid, and his wise eyes were puffy from sleep. Rowan crossed two fists over his chest and bowed to Wickham.

"I have foreseen Master Leith violating the code of apprenticeship," Rowan announced. "He is guilty of corruption in its most loathsome form. I propose we withdraw Kyler immediately from his clutches and arrest him!"

Wickham paused, sighed, and motioned for his assistant to close the great oak door behind him. Rowan dropped his hands and stood, resolute, in front of the headmaster.

"If it was a vision you saw, my boy," Wickham began, "then Leith is guilty of nothing, yet."

"The bylaws state that we can arrest a criminal before he commits the crime foreseen. . . ."

"If it has been foreseen by three trusted members of the Chamber who have earned their stripes," Wickham interrupted, "what infamy do you suppose would occur if we trusted all of our members with every vision? Someone in a jealous rage, for example," the headmaster said, looking knowingly at the young man. "He might fabricate a vision for his own personal satisfaction. For this reason, I could not send my officers after Leith based on the divination of one student."

"But I know it to be true!" Rowan persisted. "He's a criminal, Headmaster. He should be brought to justice."

"And you wish to send your scribe friend to the dungeons, as well?" Wickham asked calmly.

Rowan blinked. "What?"

"You realize if she is a willing participant, she will be punished with her master. Her stripes will be taken, and she will serve a sentence in the dungeon with more putrid creatures than Master Leith, I can assure you." Wickham rounded the desk to face the boy. "I am the most highly decorated soothsayer in Salyndria, Rowan," he said. "Don't think I haven't sensed your affection for the girl. I know you are aggrieved that she does not return it, but this is not the way to remedy your frustration."

Rowan swallowed. "Headmaster, if we do not take action . . ."

"You have my answer," Wickham said, then waved a hand at the door. It eased open, light pouring in from the hallway. "Now, get some rest."

The boy took a moment, staring out the window at the moonlit landscape. With an aggravated huff, he exited. The door closed behind him, and he stood in the hallway. The assistant that guarded the headmaster's quarters nodded politely at him. Rowan grimaced, then marched away.

CHAPTER FIVE

THE GLAMOUR

Leith pulled a thick book from the shelf and crossed the laboratory. He tossed it on the table in front of Kyler.

"Transformation," he said.

Kyler eyed him. "Pardon, my lord?" she replied, looking confused.

Leith answered her by placing one hand over the book, his long, black sleeve brushing the table. He opened his mouth to speak.

"Modifus," he said firmly.

Quickly and fluidly, the cover turned hard and gray. The corners turned round and smooth, and the pages dissolved. In only seconds, the book became a stone, flat and square-shaped like the ones in the courtyard. Kyler reached out and touched its surface. It was damp with melted snow.

"How . . . how did you . . .?" she began.

"You must draw from an object you have already seen, something you are very familiar with. If you choose to transform it into a thing you don't know well, you'll end up with a warped, unconvincing result. And," Leith explained, pausing as the stone gently changed back into a book, "the basic spell only lasts a moment. Now, you," he said, and gestured at the book.

Kyler looked up at him. "You jest, master," she replied in a laugh.

Leith met her eyes, his lids half-closed in stoic disregard. "Never," he answered. "Choose your form," he said.

"That's impossible!" she told him. "You've given me advanced spells before, but transformation is for exalted sorcerers, heads of the Academy! You can't possibly expect me . . ."

"Your flagrant outbursts waste our time!" Leith roared back, slamming a fist on the table, making the book leap. Kyler stepped backward. "I told you on the first day you arrived," he said in a quieter, deadlier voice. He had to temper himself if he wanted her to comply. "You'll do as I instruct and you won't question me. Choose your form."

Kyler hesitated. "No, Master," she replied. "I won't disobey the Academy."

There was a cold silence in the room. Leith was quiet for a moment. Of course, she was loyal to the core. He would have to get creative. He sneered at her and stood back.

"I see," he said. "And what has the Academy given you to make you reject an opportunity such as this?" he asked. "In only a matter of weeks, your magic has flourished remarkably. The Academy," he said the word bitterly, "was too inept to instruct you properly. They threw you in a basement with a pile of dank manuscripts and told you to look to the past, not the future."

"I am grateful they allowed me robes at all," Kyler shot back.

"Be grateful that you were sent to me!" Leith growled. "The rules of the Academy are a cage. The rules have kept a gifted sorceress like you buried in a mountain of parchment. This," he said, snatching up her ink-stained fingers and raising them to her, "is capable of so much more than your loyalty forbids."

"The archives are my passion," Kyler protested, yanking her hand away.

"Reading about the adventures and accomplishments of others is the closest you've come to living the life you've always dreamed of," Leith countered quickly.

Kyler halted. "What do you mean?"

Leith turned his back to her and crossed the room to fetch a decorated dagger that lay on a smaller table. He took it up and turned to show it to her. The dim afternoon sunlight that seeped in through the crack in the drapes played on the short steel blade as he pulled it from its sheath. The ringing of the metal as it left the leather resonated.

"The battles and travels of every sorcerer you study must leave you with tremendous longing," Leith explained, holding the blade up to the light and examining it. "As a historian, you are able to roam Salyndria through the legends you narrate. But," he said, looking past the blade at her, "long ago, someone declared you unworthy of adventure. If I were to tell you otherwise, would you be willing to sacrifice that chance to prove your loyalty to an institution that denied you your destiny?"

Kyler did not answer. Her eyes were on the blade. Leith saw that he may have made his case, even if only for the moment. He had to make the most of the opportunity. He motioned her to come to him. With great apprehension, Kyler moved toward him, her gaze on the dagger he held, its sharp point aimed at the ceiling. She stopped in front of him. Leith placed his hand over the dagger's point.

"Imagine an enemy arrow or spear, the end of a sword," he began, using his academic voice once more. "Imagine if you could change it into something harmless just before it reached you. Modifus," he said.

The dagger immediately began to mutate into a small, dull twig, like the ones from the trees outside. Leith held the twig in his hand, showing it to her. Kyler reached out to touch it.

"Careful," Leith said sternly, as her hand closed around it. Kyler took her hand away just before the twig changed back into a dagger. Leith flipped it in his fingers, held it by the blade and reached the hilt out to her. "Now you," he said again.

Kyler's eyes flicked up from the blade to him. "Master, please do not ask this of me."

"Shall I remind you that you have already performed a prohibited spell that left a rare artifact in ruin on this floor?" Leith snapped. "At least, this time, you are only following orders," he said.

She paused, looked down at the dagger, then took it in one hand. She placed the other hand inches above its point, palm-side down. He could see the concentration on her face as she tried to think of something she was familiar with.

"Modifus," she said.

The blade was unchanged. Kyler opened her eyes. She looked up at Leith and shook her head.

"Again," he ordered.

She shut her eyes once more. He tried to imagine what item in her mind would be harmless. What would she choose?

"Modifus," she repeated, her voice sounding daunted.

This was his chance. Leith lurched forward suddenly and seized both her hands with incredible force.

"Master!" she cried. "What are you doing?"

She tried to pull away from him, but he gripped his fingers around hers over the hilt, while his other hand hooked her wrist above the blade.

"Concentrate," Leith told her calmly as he held her hand steady above the point. "Magic does not respond to weakness. You must rouse it. Choose your form!"

"I can't! Please let me go. Please!" Kyler exclaimed, pulling at his hold. She was stronger than he imagined. Leith slowly inched her hand toward the dagger's point.

"You can," said Leith calmly. "And you will."

Just then, Leith jerked her hand toward the point, where it pricked the center of her palm. Kyler flinched.

"Stop!" she pleaded, resisting him. "Please, stop!" He held the dagger poised less than an inch away from her hand. Leith pressed from both ends, driving the blade slowly closer. "Please," she said again in a sob.

Kyler shut her eyes, warm tears streaming down her cheeks. Leith held his grip, watching her face. After a few seconds, he recognized it, that slow, growing flame of strength a sorcerer feels just before a spell comes alive. Her clenched jaw slowly relaxed, and her conflicted expression softened. Her breathing slowed.

"Modifus," she said.

The dagger under her fingers was no longer a dagger. It was an empty cup, one like he'd seen long ago at the Chamber of Sight at banquets. Kyler's hands were shaking in his. He released her. She stared down at the empty cup, realizing what she had done.

"By Nythos," Kyler said in a whisper.

She held the cup at eye-level to examine it more closely, her mouth gaped open and her eyes still wet with tears. Her amazement dimmed as she glanced up at Leith. Kyler quickly looked down at the other hand, seeing at once the tiny red punctures and scratches that decorated her palm.

"You have little faith in yourself," Leith told her, walking forward.

Kyler backed away. "Don't touch me," she ordered, the cup still hanging by its handle in her other hand.

"Kyler," Leith said, continuing toward her. "Let me explain."

She turned to flee, but he caught her and whirled her around to face him, gripping her by the shoulders. With a surprising amount of force, she gave him a shove, breaking away. He stumbled back, looking at her in alarm. Leith hadn't yet seen his apprentice so outraged. The hazel eyes glared at him. She looked down at her hand once more. The cup had turned back to its original form, but not as he'd introduced it. It was the blade, but it was still in its sheath. Kyler touched the leather, her brows knitted in confusion. She suddenly looked repulsed, as if it were a dead rodent. Leith saw Kyler's grip on it tighten, then suddenly, she hurled it at his feet with a shout of frustration.

Kyler stormed out of the laboratory, her quiet sobs still echoing. Leith reached down to pick it up. He took a deep breath and pulled it out of the sheath. He frowned as he examined his reflection in its steel.

"That went well," he said cynically to himself.

It was late when Leith woke that night, stirred by the howling wind outside his window. He grumbled, raking back his hair. Moonlight illuminated the whirling snow and crept onto his antique canopied bed. He sat up and threw off the covers. There were no candles in his bedroom, only a chandelier caked with dust and cobwebs. His eyes lit the rest of the room with a blue glow, and he pulled on a robe over his bare chest and black breeches.

There were books stacked on a cluttered writing desk in the corner, one larger than the rest with black leather binding and silver lettering. There were jars and containers on shelves, much like his study, and several decorative incense vessels were perched by his bedside with herbs known for their tranquilizing qualities. Several hooks held his robes, cloaks, and powder pouches.

Leith stared out the window, looking down at the yard below and the dark woods beyond. Their voices called to him some nights— whispering, pleading for resurrection. It wouldn't be long now. Just then, a light caught his eye, down in a window on the first floor. The library. Her shadow could be seen at the window through wind-tossed snow. It seemed he wasn't the only one who slept poorly. Leith left the window and made his way downstairs.

Two torches burned at the far end of the room. Leith heard pages turning as he entered. He slipped down to the end of the aisle and rounded the corner. Kyler sat in the desk chair, her knees bundled at her chest and covered by a long white gown and gray robe. Her unending brown tresses lay about her shoulders, like the curling vines on the courtyard wall. He noticed that one hand had a strip of cloth tied around it, where the dagger had "pricked" her. He was somewhat dismayed to see her studying a section on transport conduits.

"They can be quite dangerous for a beginner," he cautioned.

Kyler gasped, jumped, then exhaled with relief. She looked down at the book. After only a second, she stiffened and squared her shoulders, then closed the book and stood up. She looked up at him, her expression remote.

"I was just leaving," she told him.

There it was. Like a cloud over the moon, a dark shadow crossed her eyes the moment she uttered the words, then vanished. Kyler was lying. She stiffly gathered up the books.

"If there is something you wish to say to me, apprentice," Leith prompted calmly, "now is the time."

Kyler stopped, then turned to him, books gathered at her chest and her body rigid with angst.

"All right," she said, then dropped the stack with a loud bang. "I have done nothing but devote myself to my studies," she began. "I have obeyed your every instruction, endured every criticism. I have done my best to atone for my every misstep, and I've endured for much longer than your previous students—don't think I'm ignorant of that. And yet you still insist on manipulating and insulting me."

She was gaining momentum now. "Do you think I don't know what kind of master you are? Do you think I wanted to study under you? Trust me, my lord, I am no happier to be here than you are to have me. This is no coveted retreat. This is a cold, bleak place where everything is dry and dead," she continued, waving her hand at the window. "Since I've arrived, I've been mocked, questioned, haunted, and deceived," she said, counting the crimes on her fingers. "Your fossil of a witch looks at me at dinner as if she waits eagerly to chop me to bits and make a stew of my limbs. I'm so sick to death of plume root that I would rather eat bat droppings, and, for the love of Amaleus, would it kill you to light a few more candles in this place?"

Leith crossed his arms and leaned on the shelf, wondering how many times she had rehearsed this speech.

"Are you finished?" he asked her.

The girl's cheeks were bright pink. She made a noticeable effort to collect herself, the linen gown heaving with her chest, briefly drawing Leith's gaze to the shadow of ample breasts beneath. She spoke with a lofty tone.

"I suppose I am," she answered.

"I am disappointed," he began, looking at her levelly. "After discovering the vitality of your own magic, you can focus on nothing but the inconveniences I've caused you."

"*Inconveniences!*" Kyler yelled, but retreated as Leith's index finger snaked up to quiet her.

"Give me your hand," he said, reaching out to her.

Kyler didn't respond. Leith let out an annoyed breath and stepped toward her.

"Don't *touch* me!" she said, backing away from him.

Leith grabbed the bandaged hand and pulled her toward him. He twisted her wrist to expose her palm and pulled off the cloth, showing her that the marks were gone. Kyler froze, perplexed.

"A glamour," Leith said softly. "I never took the knife from the sheath."

"What?" she asked.

"I had to make you believe you were in danger. It was the only way," he said. "How can I teach you if you won't trust me?" he asked.

"Why should I trust you?" Kyler said.

"How many other masters have failed you?" Leith said. "How many times have you passed the restricted spell books, wishing you could pluck one without consequence? Have I not provided you with these freedoms? Have I not been a faithful instructor? Tell me, girl," he said, releasing her hand, "what great disservice have I done you besides give you what your precious Academy wouldn't?"

"You can afford to ignore the regulations," she told him. "They favor you. They need you. What leverage have I when I stand before the Council for the spells I've learned here?"

Leith laughed aloud. "You confound me, scribe!" he said. "All your years of yearning, watching your classmates earn their robes while you wallow in self-doubt. When you finally uncover your own power, you can do nothing but worry about trivial mandates." He began to circle her slowly. "Imagine ten years from now, when you are assigned some menial military task like casting a sleeping spell over the enemy or levitating soldiers over a wall. You'll remember what you could have been, what legacy you might have left, were you shrewd enough to embrace it." Leith stopped at her shoulder, his mouth at her ear. "You'll no longer be plagued by your aspirations," he whispered. "Only your regrets."

"I don't have to listen to this," Kyler replied, and fled toward the library door.

"Kyler," Leith called, as if he'd dropped something and was burdened to have to pick it up again. "Kyler!" he called out again.

She sprinted for the door, but his spell was quick. With only a small flick of his hand, the door slammed shut, the click of the lock echoing. The torch flame danced. Kyler stopped. Her slim figure stood in the aisle, draped in willowy gray and white fabric. There was the outline of sleek thighs in the folds as she turned back, a soft crease where her legs came together.

"What do you want from me?" she demanded to know.

Leith approached her, standing over her so closely that he could feel the heat of her body. The gown sat low on her neck, the medallion resting on smooth, even skin.

"Can't you understand?" he said. "You are gifted with so much more than magic," he told her, reaching up to brace her jaw in one hand. She winced. "Had I thought less of you, I'd have you climb your way up with petty charms, trivial potions, and curses. But, you're worth more to me than that. Never have I felt such pride in any student until now, and never have I felt more regret than for having misjudged you."

Kyler met his eyes. Just then, the torch that lit the room waned dramatically. Leith looked up. His sight suddenly outlined the darkened room in blue. There was only a faint glow of torch light coming from behind the shelves. Under his fingers, he felt her jaw clench. Lust inhibits sorcery.

"Did you light that torch with your magic?" he asked after a moment.

He could tell she held her breath. "No, my lord," she said on her exhale. "I brought a torch with me," she said shakily. Even in the dim light, the shadow came again, a dark shade over her eyes like something flying overhead. "I should get to sleep," said Kyler. She was trembling now. "Could you unlock the door, master?"

Leith's hand was still on her cheek. She'd lied. Her magic had failed her, and he knew why. He paused, then released her.

"It is in your power," he reminded mildly, gesturing to the door. "You've practiced the counter spell many times."

Kyler delayed, looking at the door, then back at her master. There was a great, impossible quandary in her eyes. She composed herself. "Of course," she said, then moved forward a pace toward the door. Slowly raising her hand and lingering a second in desperate silence, she spoke. "Ostium Libertus," she said. The library was mute. Only the muffled sound of the snowstorm outside and the faint chirping of bats echoed. The door was unchanged. "Ostium Libertus," Kyler repeated, her voice halting.

Her spell failed again. Leith was amused as he listened to her repeat the words once more. The heavy door remained closed and locked. Finally, the sorcerer had his fill. He reached out for her.

"Enough," came his warm whisper in her ear.

He took her shoulders in his grip and squeezed with fretful urgency, covering her neck with fierce kisses as if he knew he was about to be ripped from a sweet dream. She heaved in his grasp, arching her back and taking in a full, astonished breath. Her pulse throbbed under his lips. In a quick, thorough movement, he spun her around and steadied her against the wall. Kyler surrendered, clutching at his robe and groping at his chest, her face upturned.

His lips finally met hers, and he kissed her like a man dying of thirst, forced to take small drops from a vial. She welcomed him, her mouth a warm, waiting refuge from the cold, listless prison his life had become. The hands that cast a thousand spells of death and suffering were at her slender waist, eager and curious as they explored and traveled upward. She shuddered when his hand found her breast, soft and full in his palm, the peak rigid even under the thick fabric of the gown.

He was lost in his malaise, the girl's exquisite body so docile in his embrace. She was soft, innocent, and inviting. He had considered himself a disciplined man, trained and seasoned in all aspects of his art. But those eyes blazing up at him choked his logic; the taste of her mouth took reason from him. He kissed her again, but suddenly, she arrested him.

Kyler's hands that were clutching at his chest were now pushing against it. He found himself taking another kiss from her, but she clenched her fists around his robe and hurled him back, his lips torn from hers.

Leith stumbled back. She said nothing. She stood against the wall, looking at the space she'd made between them instead of his eyes. She was catching her breath, and one of her delicate hands was weakly outstretched toward him in a halting gesture, her fingers splayed and trembling. He could feel his own pulse throbbing in his head. He made himself stand still and keep his distance from her. He tried to read her face as she slowly lowered her hand. Kyler's eyes were wrecked with what looked like a mix of anguish and exasperation.

She finally looked up at him. He saw her throat constrict with a swallow.

"Open the door," came her voice, low and serious.

At her words, the world came sharply back into focus. The world that had seemed their own tragically became once more the world where Wickham lived. Leith was acutely aware of the heat leaving his veins. Kyler was rigid against the Cognitite, closing up her robe around her chest and shoulders in a swift motion. She cast her eyes at the floor.

"Kyler," came his throaty reply.

"Open it."

He looked at her a moment more, savoring her beauty in the torch light, which was once again bright. He waved a hand at the door, and with a click and a creak, it opened.

Kyler stepped away from the wall and moved toward it. Leith raised his hand to stop her.

"I'll go," he said. At this, she met his eyes. "Good night, Kyler."

Leith exited, leaving Kyler once more alone in the library.

The door flew open as Leith came storming into his study. He hadn't bothered with a conduit, nor had it even occurred to him. He streaked over to the wine and sloppily poured himself a cup. Marisele stood in the corner, looming over the silver basin and gripping the rim with her shriveled hands. She glared at him with her only eye.

"You fool!" she spat. Leith ignored her, gulping down the wine in one swallow and immediately pouring himself more. She moved toward him.

"You irreverent insect! Aren't the whores from the Academy enough to sate you? You could have ruined everything!" she howled, then raised a hand to strike him.

Leith whirled to catch her wrist in his hand, seizing it with such force that she let out a cry of pain. He gripped her neck with the other and looked at her evenly. "You dare assault me, prune?" he replied wickedly. "You forget your place. Perhaps you should like to go back there, to the twisted black tree where you nursed your cowardice!" With that, he pushed her away from him.

The old witch stumbled back and coughed, grasping at her throat. "Recedeo!" he shouted, raising a hand up toward the basin, which abruptly drained of water. "The girl is under control. You've no more need to keep *an eye* on us," he said, and retired to his room, slamming his door.

CHAPTER SIX

LUNATHYL

The morning was quiet and cold. What little sunlight that crept in through the library window had woken Kyler. The previous night came washing over her, piercing the remnants of dreams. She sat up in the bed, looking out the window at the fallen snow that covered the courtyard floor. Her eyes were crusted with dried tears, and they stung from the light. She had not wanted to return to her cell, so she had crawled up into the library's bed where she cried herself to sleep.

Kyler slipped out of bed and took up her robe, which hung over the desk chair. She pulled it tight around her and shivered, looking around at the dim bookshelves. The books she had dropped were still in a stack, but the one that sat on top was not the one she recalled. *How to Master the Transport Conduit* had been on the bottom. She wiped her eyes and combed through her hair with her fingers.

She fought back the images that once more ignited her: the cobalt light sapped from Leith's eyes when he pressed her against the wall, the warmth of his body . . . she couldn't remember anything she wanted more, except magic. Still, she shut her eyes and tried to shake it from her mind. Rowan's words about Leith's reputation resonated, and the bitter wave of shame washed over her.

Just then, she realized it wasn't morning after all, as she gazed out the window at the sun, which had passed the apex of the sky. She hurried out of the library, through the empty common room and up the stairway. Halting at the archway, she saw that the laboratory was dark, the curtains drawn, with no sign that anyone had been there. Puzzled, she washed her face in the lavatory and closed herself inside her cell.

She dressed quickly, shedding the night dress and pulling on the brown robe with the ink stain. She tied back her hair and gathered up her books, trying to behave as if there had been no disturbance in her education whatsoever. Perhaps if she could, he would as well. Kyler made her way to the lab, set her books down, and pulled open the curtains. The afternoon light poured in. She wandered about in silence, running her fingers over the containers and wooden boxes on the long table. Finally, she found a stool and propped herself up on it. Kyler waited.

After what seemed like hours, she closed the book she had been pretending to read and gave a weighty sigh. How could he leave her to wonder? Had something happened to him? Did the Chamber of Sight detect his crime, and this was some peculiar test of her loyalty? Kyler hopped off the stool. She would not continue through the winter this way. She had to speak to him; she had to tell him it was a mistake, and that it would not be allowed to happen again. She came to earn her robes, not be seduced by a lustful and ruthless sorcerer. She left the laboratory, tracked the hall, and climbed the steps to the third floor.

The sun was fading outside the small windows of the stairway, and her heart leapt in her chest as she neared the heavy oak door that closed off her master's chambers. Kyler knew she would not be welcome, but she had to confront him. She knocked twice. The sound resonated like a drum throughout the narrow stone shaft. She placed her ear against the door, but could hear only the sound of faint bubbling and a crackling fire. She knocked again, then hovered one hand in front of the lock.

"Ostium Libertus," she chanted quietly. She was surprised when the lock clicked open and the door drifted ajar. "Hello?" she called, pushing the door open farther. A weak flame housed inside a clouded glass lantern sat on a desk. There was a small, blackened hearth where a fire danced. "Master?" she called out.

The room was unoccupied. Marisele was nowhere to be seen. The study was cluttered with books and magical trinkets, grotesque organs and animal limbs in jars, bowls of rune stones, and bottles of powder. Kyler cautiously stepped inside. There were two doors on opposite sides of the study. She imagined that each closed off her master's and Marisele's sleeping chambers. There was a beaker of liquid bubbling over a green flame, behaving in a way she had never seen before. It was upside-down, the bubbles dropping down inside instead of rising up. Kyler frowned at it, then crossed the room to one of the doors.

She raised her hand to knock, but thought better of it. Instead, she put her ear to the door. A loud, rickety snore erupted from behind the wood, followed by a high-pitched moan. Startled, she lurched backward. It was Marisele's room. She was suddenly very afraid, as if she'd wandered into a cave full of sleeping bears. She backed into the desk where the lantern sat, then whirled to steady it as it swayed. She waited a moment to listen.

It seemed she hadn't disturbed anyone. Kyler let out a sigh of relief. As she took her hands from the lantern, the light revealed a large black book with silver letters resting near it. A chill claimed her spine, and her lips parted in shock. The letters were hardly letters at all. They were ancient symbols, the alphabet of the Black Trade, which she had learned in order to translate some of the older archives. The symbols spelled Doctrines of Iniquity. This was no ordinary text. It was a Grimoire—a book of dark spells!

Something moved. Kyler's eyes flicked up at the open study door. She swallowed, feeling her skin crawl at the sight of a ghostly face half-shadowed in the stairway. There was a figure outside the door: one pale hand, accented by a torn purple sleeve, clutching the wooden frame. It was the spirit from the library. Two red eyes caught the lantern light and stared at her. She took a slow step forward. As she did, the spirit withdrew to the stairs, headed upward.

"Wait!" she called quietly after it.

She followed, closing the door carefully behind her and climbing the steps two by two. It grew darker farther up, so she opened her palm, igniting a flame. Soon, she reached the top of the stairway where a dark archway loomed. It was colder, and the air grew icy in her nostrils as she stopped short. There were sounds: the fluttering of wings, chirping. An enormous room opened up in the shape of a circle with a huge rounded dome as its roof. There were no torches, no decorations or furniture—just a pile of dried-up scrolls and a large scope turned on its side, the lens cracked.

A single stream of amber sunset struck the stone floor, which was made of the same black stones as the front hall downstairs. Her flame revealed the roof that arched high above her. It was dotted everywhere with the small, compressed black figures of sleeping bats. A few of the bats were awake, flitting from one side of the dome to the other with curiosity. Before she knew what had happened, she nearly stumbled over a slight rise in the floor. She looked down at it.

It was a circle, projected a few inches high and bearing the seal of the Astronomer's Guild. It was positioned right below the dome's opening, where the scope must have once sat. She knelt to examine it further, her flame illuminating its carvings and symbols. She recognized it from her reading and ran her fingers over the markings with fascination. Her attention was thwarted, however, by an overzealous bat that suddenly soared down at her, then swooped up again. Kyler ducked and covered her head, her flame snuffing out. She looked up again, eyeing the now darkened dome for any more figures flying low. The sun was nearly gone, its orange light turning a soft purple.

Kyler had almost resolved to abandon her enterprise, but halted as she stood before the seal. There was something different about it now. There, in the darkness, were alternate letters carved in a white, pearl-like stone that glowed like the light of the moon.

"Flame," she commanded, bringing her light back to her hand. Instantly, the letters vanished, showing her the seal she had first seen. Kyler closed her hand, making the room dark again. The letters reappeared, pale and luminescent against the shadows. "Lunathyl," Kyler whispered to herself, touching the stone with awe.

She recognized it as the rare stone used in the spire of the Chamber of Light to lead the wounded in the dark. But it couldn't be, she thought. Lunathyl was only discovered a hundred and fifty years ago, and the observatory had been abandoned much longer than that. Kyler realized with dreadful certainty that this was an addition, and one not likely sanctioned by the Academy. Her heart pounded as she read the white letters that encompassed the outskirts of the seal in a circular form. *Here seek the way that leads to our slumbering Lord.*

Kyler clapped a hand over her mouth.

Malantheus!

It must have been his followers who altered the seal. But it wasn't a seal anymore. It was a conduit, disguised and hidden from any visitors to the observatory. The symbols would never have been seen. Anyone who ventured into this room would have carried a torch with them. Except for . . .

"Leith," Kyler said aloud.

The bats stirred above her, several more of them coming awake as the sunlight faded more quickly. Kyler's pulse raced, her blood flowing hot in her veins as the events of the winter flashed before her in a collage of evidence against her master—the question of her loyalty, the collection of Malantheus's history, and his possession of a Grimoire. She rose from the floor, staring down at the outline of Lunathyl that seemed to call to her. She was angry, confused, and afraid—but most of all, she was curious. Kyler stepped up onto the seal, her face taking on the shadow of the night as the last ray of sun disappeared behind the black trees. She shut her eyes and held her breath, not knowing what exactly to expect. She braced herself, and in another second, she disappeared.

Kyler's face twisted with pain as she found herself face-down on the floor, feeling as if a hundred books were stacked on her chest. She couldn't quite tell what had happened; she knew only that there was dirt under her tingling fingers, and that her head ached terribly. The transport was like being suddenly crushed between two stone slabs in one second, then released in the next. She realized she wasn't breathing and opened her mouth to take in a wheezing gasp. She coughed harshly several times and groaned as she lifted herself, crawling backward into a seated position against a wall. It was too dark to know where she was. The only light came from several fist-sized openings just over her head. An identical circle of Lunathyl letters glowed a few feet away on the ground.

All she could hear was a hollow drip, the sound echoing as if in a tunnel. Kyler strained to place her hand in front of her and called her flame. Abruptly, her surroundings were revealed: an underground passageway, the walls made of rock and damp dirt, standing wide and rounded. The burrow vanished into darkness at the edges of her firelight, and behind her was a barricade of boulders where the conduit lay. Through its tiny openings she saw more of the passage. There was a sharp streak of light shooting through the darkness on the other side.

The well, she thought. She realized she must be just below the courtyard.

She took a moment to recover, closing her eyes as her head throbbed with pain. Finally, she stood, holding the light out in front of her, and began to walk. As she trekked forward, she noticed the metallic powder on her brown robes and slapped it away with her free hand. The passage opened up here and there to wider parts overrun with roots. Soon after, the tunnel gave way to dirt again, this time teeming with plume root, a thousand large violet buds sticking out of the walls. They were everywhere, bright green tufts like down feathers projecting from the ends of each.

"So this is where we get our stew," Kyler said, shining her flame over them.

She continued through the tunnel, the roots adorning the walls for another hundred feet. After that, they narrowed into rock. It seemed she walked for miles. The rock grew darker in color the farther she traveled, and the passage seemed to gradually slope downward. She had been using one hand for her fire and one to brace herself against one wall, but suddenly she felt running water on the rock. Kyler stopped to examine it. Sure enough, there was a trickling stream that followed the cracks in the wall down to the floor. She was underneath the coastline.

Kyler picked up her pace, making her way down the empty tunnel as it grew still narrower. The only sound was the ever-increasing water flow on the rock walls. At last, she stopped short. The passage gaped before her into a large, circular chamber. There was a mound of old mining tools next to a make-shift platform that extended to the ceiling. Kyler held her light up to the roof, exposing a deep, jagged depression perfectly centered in the midst of four more glowing Lunathyl symbols. As she slowly advanced toward it, a sound like she'd never heard pierced the silent darkness.

It was an agonized howling, like a woman screaming during childbirth. Kyler stepped back from the platform, her eyes wide in horror.

"Don't worry," a voice said. Kyler jumped, trying to find its source in the dark corners of the chamber. "They don't know we're here."

Kyler spotted two glowing blue spheres in the shadows. Leith stepped into the light. He wore only his breeches, his broad chest and muscled arms slick with sweat and smeared in some places with dirt. His black hair was swept back and damp, and he held a chisel in one hand. He took another step forward.

"Don't come any closer!" Kyler barked, turning her head briefly to eye the tunnel behind her for a quick escape. "What have you done?" she asked him. "What is this place?"

Leith's expression was dull. He showed no sign that he was surprised to see her there. He held the chisel lazily. "You don't disappoint, apprentice," he said. "I had a feeling you'd find your way here, although I'm sorry about the conduit. Your first time shouldn't be unguided. I'll wager it knocked the wind right out of you," he said, grinning.

"You led me here," Kyler said stoically. "You left me a trail."

Leith sighed. "Your insatiable curiosity and eye for detail led you here. I planted suggestions."

"The conduit book," she said with sudden realization. "You moved it to the top of the stack."

"Stop pretending that you were acting under pretense," he scoffed. "No one forced you to read it. No one forced you to come looking for me or to nose around the observatory." He tossed the chisel once in his hand. "You could have spent the afternoon reading in your room."

"Why not let me? Why did you lead me here, instead?" she said.

She was guarded and cold in her tone, hoping to convey indifference. She wanted him to see that she was finished being dutiful and polite. He had gotten the better of her emotions; he tried to take advantage of her desire for approval. She would not be fooled into letting him affect her again.

"It served a few purposes. For one, to see how keen you are," he said. "I certainly didn't think you'd see the Lunathyl, though I know you're one of few who would be able to decipher it," he said, pointing briefly at her with the chisel. "Most of all, we both know you'd discover what I'm doing here sooner or later. Rather than conduct my work in secret, you can see and judge for yourself. You will no longer wonder about my motivations."

"Where are we?" Kyler said matter-of-factly.

"The secret passage to Lamentiose."

"They searched the grounds for a passage, but nothing was found."

"Of course not. The passage was filled with water, then. A simple receding spell would have emptied it, but the Academy underestimated the magical prowess of the Black Trade," he explained, tossing the chisel onto the platform. "That, and it was unfinished. I've spent much of my time here picking up where they left off. Now, I'm nearly through."

"Nearly through," Kyler repeated, then looked up. "We're below Lamentiose?"

"Below Lamentiose, yes, but more importantly," said Leith, "directly below Malantheus's crypt. They marked it," he told her, pointing at the runes.

"How could they have marked it if it wasn't yet complete?" Kyler asked with suspicion. "Object projection is an outlawed spell, found only in the ancient Grimoires," she said.

"Yes," he admitted, answering her accusatory tone. "I have one in my possession."

"But they took it from you when you were arrested," Kyler said.

"They took an ordinary spell book," he told her, reaching up to grip the platform's frame. "I placed a glamour on it, and they never suspected a thing. I knew they were only going to bury it away in some archive vault and never touch it again. If they were to look now, they would find *Basic Vanishing Spells, Volume Two*."

"You're plotting to resurrect him," Kyler said.

"No," Leith answered, almost laughing. "The spells sealing him are too ancient and powerful for any sorcerer living to bring him back. I only seek his gauntlet. Malantheus was the only one who nearly fashioned a world where sorcery reigns. This is as it should be. I'll resurrect his army of followers, command them to march on the closest branch of the Academy, and overthrow the Order."

"The Chamber of Sight," Kyler guessed.

"Yes. After that, it should be fairly easy to enlist the help of the seers in order to sweep across the kingdom. I don't think they'll be too heartbroken to see the soldiers murdered. Salyndria's military has never been warm to sorcerers of any branch. They treat us like caged rats. They took great pleasure in torturing me after my capture."

"It's impossible," Kyler argued. "The island is made up of impenetrable rock. Once you dig through to its foundation, nothing exists that can break it except . . ."

"Dragon's blood," Leith interrupted. "Which has been boiling in my study."

Kyler was quiet. The shrieking echoed once more. She shuddered. "People will be killed. I can't let you do this," she said.

"I'm afraid it isn't a matter of earning your permission," Leith said dully.

She hated his nonchalance, hated how he spoke about taking over the kingdom as if it were reorganizing a bookshelf. Most of all, she hated his impersonal, smug manner, as if it were her first day at the observatory and he had no regard for her at all.

"You can't keep me here," she said.

"I can," he answered. "But, even if it wasn't in my power, the spirits are too taken with you to let you leave. Besides, I can't have you and your stubborn devotion flying off to warn Headmaster Wickham. By the time he foresees all of this, the spirits of Solemn Woods will be advancing on the Chamber," Leith said, bending down to pick up several of his tools. "Once my plan is engaged, I'll release you. I only hope you'll heed that sensibility of yours and join my cause."

"So, you do plan to exploit me," Kyler said. "I didn't come here to be your pawn—or share your bed. I was sent here to learn magic."

"It isn't me who wishes to exploit you. Not anymore," he admitted. "It was Wickham. You were sent here to distract me," Leith quietly corrected.

Kyler halted. "What?"

"Think on it: you know it to be true. Wickham had his plans for you, and it had nothing to do with improving your craft," Leith said, placing the tools on the platform. "He wanted to divert my attention, and who better suited than a beautiful scribe who would be a challenge to instruct?"

Kyler stared at him, her eyes suddenly blurring with tears. "You're lying," she choked out through clenched teeth.

As Leith shook his head slowly from side to side, her eyes drifted absently—remembering, realizing. The honest brow was abruptly bent, and her face revealed the agony of betrayal. She shut her eyes against her tears and turned away, desperate not to let him see. Without a word, Kyler turned and ran.

"Kyler," he called after her.

She rushed down the tunnel, her flame jumping and unruly in her palm, hoping he wouldn't use a spell to stop her. She blinked away angry tears, gripping the hem of her robes with one hand and moving quickly through the rock until it became dirt once more. Kyler stopped briefly.

"Omnia Ignatus!" she commanded harshly.

Her flame leapt from her hand, and there was a sound like black powder being thrown onto a hearth. The old sconces lining the rest of the tunnel burst alive with fire. Kyler continued with a deliberate pace, running past the walls of plume root, past the last of the torches until finally, she met the conduit. Stepping onto it, undaunted, she closed her eyes and vanished.

Kyler was spit out into the observatory's dome, and she groaned as she fell forward onto the floor. The bats were awake all around her, swooping down and up again. Getting to her feet, she flinched and shielded herself from them.

"Omnia Mitigo!" Kyler shouted at them.

Within seconds, the bats retreated to the ceiling, folding themselves up into sleep. Kyler nursed her head with one hand and forced her weakened legs to carry her out through the archway, down the darkened staircase, and out to the second-floor balcony. The front door required a spell beyond her power, but there was one she could use. She climbed up onto the railing.

"Descendum," she said, and stepped off.

Kyler floated down to the courtyard floor, where her boots hit the ground hard. She made her way over to the stable. She rushed Pherylon out through the stone passage and mounted him. She rode out onto the misted grounds and made her way to the gate. The air was like ice in her throat as she called out a command that swung it open and pulled her hood up as they passed through. Already, the voices were at her ear. The gnarled black branches loomed overhead, and she urged Pherylon into a gallop down the dark trail. Figures flitted in the corner of her sight, wearing robes of red, white, black, and purple, moving frantically between the trees.

Kyler kept her eyes on the trail, despite the hissing and whispering that quickly surrounded her. "You can't keep me here!" she screamed.

A figure then appeared on the trail ahead, a corpse of a woman in a dirt-streaked white robe. Pherylon whinnied and stalled. Kyler blinked and the woman was gone. The whispers grew louder as Kyler jerked her head from side to side, turning her horse around in a circle with suspicion. The woods were empty. She turned back toward the trail, where the woman reappeared, this time directly in front of Pherylon. Treacherous red irises stared vacantly up at Kyler, as the ghost grinned and shrieked.

Pherylon sprang backward, lifting his front hooves from the ground. Kyler cried out and fell from the saddle. She landed hard on her shoulder, rolling over quickly to see half a dozen grotesque figures bearing down on her. They came from nowhere, of all ages and from all four Orders, their eyes like blood and their faces like chalk.

"No!" she cried, trying to crawl away, but the visions had already begun.

She braced her arms out in front of her, but still she saw the victims. The murders came in flashes—a young woman run through with a sword, blood dripping from her lips. There was a group of soldiers, their eyes being ripped from their sockets. "No!" Kyler screamed again as more spirits surrounded her. She saw an old man being burned alive, his body engulfed in flames. She heard him wailing in agony. They showed her his melting flesh, his wrinkled face as it turned to ash.

"Abscido!" a grating voice broke in.

At once, the visions subsided, and Kyler could see the tall shadow of a man groping at the reigns of her horse. Pherylon reared up, but the man kept his grip with one hand and held the other out to the figures that encircled them. "Abscido!" the voice shouted again. The figures recoiled, turning from Kyler to whom she could only guess was her master. They writhed toward him, growling and hissing. She tried to lift herself up, cold and shaking on the cursed soil as she watched them descend upon him. Standing firm and unmoving, he let them come close.

"Leith!" Kyler called out.

Suddenly, as if prompted by her voice, the figures sprang at Leith with howls and screams, enveloping him until he was no longer visible. He had released Pherylon, who galloped away into the black trees. Only seconds later, there was a bright flash of blue flame and the figures were sent flying back as if by an explosion. Many of them vanished or retreated into shadow, but some remained, glaring with hollowed eyes.

They came at him, two and three at a time. Leith was visible now, holding a ball of blue light that cast a glow around him. He wielded it with both hands.

"Reverte!" he commanded, extending his hands out.

A blast came from the orb he directed at the figures. It knocked them back, and they shrieked with anger.

Kyler's head throbbed as she shielded herself against the battle.

Just before the world went black, before Kyler closed her eyes against the final blast of light, the last spirit vanished and the blurred figure of her master knelt close.

A lantern burned on the long table near Kyler as she sat slumped in one of the dining hall chairs. A large blanket was draped over her shoulders, her long hair damp and stringy about the sides of her face. She shivered. Leith set a large steaming goblet in front of her. Kyler straightened and pulled the blanket more snugly around her. She leaned forward to take a suspicious look at the drink.

"If I wanted you dead, it would be easier than that," Leith said. "It isn't poison. Drink it. It will help clear your mind."

"What is it?" she asked dryly.

"Better you don't know," he answered. Reluctantly, her hands emerged from the folds of the blanket and took the cup. She brought it to her lips and took a slow sip. Grimacing, she swallowed, then took another sip. "You're brave," Leith told her. "I've known others who have fallen victim to the ghosts of the woods, none returning with their sanity, let alone their lives."

Kyler drank deliberately, though she didn't like the elixir's flavor. "You could have been free of me," she said suddenly, without looking up. "Why didn't you just let them have me?"

"I'm no monster," he said. "Your fate would have been worse than death. Though you are troublesome, you are undeserving of that. The Academy would blame me, of course. I can't afford to have your blood on my conscience or my record." He paused. "I can assume your next endeavor will be to try and stop me," he added. "But it will turn out much the same way. I've had my plans long before you came here, Kyler. They will come to fruition regardless of how strongly you disapprove of them."

"Perhaps it's foolish of me," she said after another sip, "to think I know something about you, but you don't seem the kind to take well to a throne. To rule Salyndria is a heavy employment," said Kyler, her eyes still on the table. "You're the kind of man who enjoys only a meager amount of obligation."

Leith half-smiled. "Very true. If there were someone fonder of kingship who could carry out my plans, I would happily commission them. Had Malantheus gone about his task correctly to begin with, perhaps our lives would be much more rewarding." Leith said, glancing resentfully at his surroundings.

"Then you are like those before you," Kyler remarked, finally looking up. "Men who carve a path of death and suffering only to rule over a wasteland. You'll subjugate all who oppose you and breathe nothing but lies to those who follow you," she said.

"Lies like those that Headmaster Wickham told you?" Leith replied coolly. "Just before he sent you off to spend the winter alone with a criminal?"

Kyler's expression changed. She was no longer angry, but contemplating. Her green eyes shone with what was left of her tears: red and tired, but abruptly aware. She mimicked his smile. "You are not so cruel," she told him quietly. "Drowning in all those bitter shadows must still be a man who once felt loyalty to those he served, who once felt loved and admired. Surely, even you must sometimes miss the light."

From the look on his face, the words seemed to pierce him. His lips parted to respond, but his wit left him. He scooted out of his chair and stood.

"Your horse had a fright," he said, his tone cold and official. "I was able to coax him back to the stable, but I fear I am not the one he will let calm him. Finish your drink," he advised, nodding at it, "and see to him. You and I will speak more tomorrow after you are rested."

Leith quickly left the dining hall, vanishing into the darkness.

The sorcerer had not kept his word. The following day passed without a visit to the second floor at all. Once the books had ceased to keep her mind from her plight, Kyler found herself curled up at the window of the desolate laboratory. She imagined that hollowed ground beneath the cold stones of the courtyard. She imagined her master pouring over his Grimoire, studying the ritual that would wake his legion. Kyler envisioned the siege, those arrogant soldiers that loitered about the chamber meeting a terrible fate. She pictured Leith on the rickety platform deep underground, his muscles quaking under his slick, dirt-streaked skin as he struck the rock with his chisel.

She closed her eyes against the thought.

Kyler climbed down from the window ledge. It was dinnertime, but she lacked an appetite for both the cuisine and the company she had grown accustomed to. The world she knew seemed to have been turned on its side. Before the winter came to a close, Salyndria would change forever, and Kyler was powerless to act.

Night settled in, a bright moon at its heels as the hours passed. The pale light drowned the lantern on the writing desk where Kyler studied. She had crept down to the library around midnight, her attempts to sleep having failed. After plunging into a history on fire branding, a chronicle detailing the ever-changing map of Salyndria, and a condensed volume of *Storm Side Myths and Legends*, Kyler finally began to feel tired. She yawned widely and stretched, looking around. She rubbed her eyes, finally deciding that she might, indeed, be able to find slumber. She crawled into the bed and dropped the curtain around her.

"Expiro," she muttered into the pillow, as she turned over and curled up under the musty blanket. The lantern's light faded into nothing. Kyler's eyes drooped closed, and she made her slow descent into a world of dreams.

The Chamber of Shadows loomed before her. Its tall, narrow door claimed the top of the wide staircase; Kyler's mother guided her up the steps to meet it. She was a frigid, raven-haired beauty, her eyes a cold, pale green, and her hair combed back impeccably into a jeweled pin. Her mother had dressed her in a blue linen frock and drove the carriage to the mountain path. From there, the escort led them up the trail that took them to the chamber, a huge gray fortress sculpted right from the mountain itself.

Kyler stared at the doors of smooth gray stone, with carvings of violent battles and scourges adorning it. The doors opened. The Headmistress appeared in her black velvet habit with silver stripes and colorful emblems, waves of gray hair falling down past her waist. Her mother nudged her inside.

"When will you visit me?" Kyler asked.

"I can't say, my darling," her mother answered coldly, touching her cheek.

In an instant, she was gone, vanishing from the tall door as it drifted closed, shutting out the daylight. Kyler turned. The chamber had vanished, too.

Behind her was a dismal spread of dying grass shrouded in low-hanging fog. The ground was marked with massive headstones. In the distance, she could see the tops of mausoleums in an endless graveyard. She heard a shrieking echo over the land, the sound growing closer. Kyler heard the ocean, hidden somewhere beyond the fog and sweeping up against the rocks on the shoreline. The howling grew closer. Dark, haggard, human-like creatures wormed toward her from the graves, their arms long and deformed, their heads hairless and oval-shaped.

She walked backward, putting her hands over her ears to block out the sound. The Hypnogoths came closer, their skin a dark purple and withered like dried fruit. Their yellow eyes were set in flat, featureless faces with lipless dark holes for mouths that produced that hideous howl. Kyler shouted and turned to run away, but met a fate some considered worse than death. One of them had waited just behind her, meeting her eyes with its reptilian gaze. It reached out, clasping her face in its freakishly long fingers. The yellow eyes were dotted in the center with a tiny black iris that saw into her fears.

Kyler screamed, but couldn't hear her own voice. She shut her eyes, seeing once more the mangled bodies of the murdered. She saw the scarlet eyes of the spirits, their black teeth grinning down at her. She saw their victims, men and women hanging from Malantheus's gallows, necks stretched and bruised, eyes swollen and protruding from their sockets. She shook her head violently, screaming and pleading for the creature to set her free from its grip.

"Kyler!" it growled with its cavernous mouth. "It's Leith!"

Kyler's eyes shot open, warm firelight replacing the yellow eyes in her dreams. Instantly, she batted the hands at her face and kicked the covers that had twisted around her legs.

"Stop!" the familiar voice commanded. Strong hands subdued her, steadied her at the shoulders and shook her once. "Stop it, Kyler. It's me!"

At last, her surroundings came into focus. The graveyard was gone, the dusty library in its place. The curtain had been swept back, and her master sat at her bedside. Her gown had come up around her thighs.

"Leith," she whispered, clenching the collar of his open robe, tears stinging her face. "They were after me. They were everywhere! Oh, the things they showed me, the awful things . . ."

"It's all right," Leith answered softly. "You're safe."

Kyler looked past him, recalling the images. She shut her eyes, so relieved it hadn't been real. She quickly embraced him, pressing herself to him as if he'd just saved her life, her face buried at his neck.

"I saw my mother," she sobbed into his shoulder. His hand cradled her head against him, his fingers in her hair.

"Shhh. It's all right," he said again.

A moment passed in silence, a wonderful calm breaking over her as she sat nestled in his hold. For a moment, she thought she could almost feel him rocking her. Kyler pulled herself away, wiped her eyes, and looked up at him soberly.

"I'm sorry I woke you," she said.

"I was awake," he admitted, pushing back a strand of her brown hair from her eyes. "I needed a particular spell book, so I . . ." Leith began, but his words faltered.

He was staring at her now with a captivated look. She remembered the last night they had met in the library, the warmth of his body, those hands so gifted with precision and power roaming her. She'd tried to push it from her mind, to guard herself against him. She had tried not to look at him in the crypt, his naked chest and muscled arms tossing the tools about. She tried putting up her defenses, but the way he looked at her now shattered them. Kyler pushed back her logic, ignored the voice that warned her of consequences. She had been dutiful and forthright her entire life. She wanted this for herself, to explore him, to belong to him.

"Perhaps you'll sleep better if you return to your cell," Leith said. "I can make you another remedy."

Kyler blinked, then exhaled. "No, no, I'll be fine," she answered, looking down at the covers.

"You're sure," he said.

She nodded. Leith lingered a second more, then stood. "Good night, then," he said, and moved to leave.

"Wait," Kyler blurted, and her hand lurched out to seize his. Her eyes were still downcast. "Please, don't leave."

CHAPTER SEVEN

DRAGON'S BLOOD

Kyler didn't want to see his face. She wondered as she gripped his wrist in her hand what he was thinking. The seconds he spent standing there were like a lifetime to her. At last, he moved to sit back down on the bed facing her.

"What is it?" he asked.

She stared at his hand, at his long fingers with shining silver rings. She played with one, turning its band and running her thumb over its runes. Then, Kyler made herself raise her eyes. Perhaps it was the lingering malaise of her dream, or his sudden warm comfort in such a desolate, bleak place—whatever it was, Kyler found herself wanting him. The longing and loneliness she had so long repressed came to her as she lingered in that small space close to him. Never had she felt this kind of desire for anyone. She'd spent a lifetime never feeling worthy enough to take anything without an invitation. In this moment, her longing took over. She leaned forward and gently kissed his mouth, hovering there near him with her eyes closed after their lips parted. She waited blindly, feeling his breath against her cheek. She imagined he was thinking of a rejection, deciding she was frivolous, infatuated, or just confused. She flinched as his hand came up to seize her jaw, taking it so forcefully she thought he was about to push her away, as she had done to him.

Instead, he kissed her back.

His lips answered hers, so heated and hungry it frightened her. Kyler was lost in a flushed weakness, reaching up to pull the robe from his shoulders. He threw it off, his hands immediately gripping her waist and pulling her close. The torch light ebbed into a single glowing flame, casting shadows over several scars on his chest and collarbone. She met his eyes, now a startling pale blue, the spell that caused them to gleam now dissipated. There was conflict in them, his brow knitted with some silent torment as they explored her. She touched his chest, her fingers running nimbly over the hard muscles that flexed in response, the strange old scars that looked like slashes or marks from a whip. He let out a breath and closed his eyes. Leith kissed her again, placed his hands on her thighs, and hitched the gown up further before plunging his hand between her legs.

Kyler surged at the touch, gasping loudly as he reached his fingers under the meager canopy of the gown. She took in quick breaths matched with harsh exhales as he worked, reaching an arm around his shoulder to hold herself to him. He caressed her fluidly and masterfully, until she was slick and quivering in his arms. A bittersweet craving made her groan and cling to him, her hips timidly matching him.

Suddenly, it attacked her, a barbed rapture that made her whole body seize. She cried out against his cheek. His other hand was around her back, bridling her as he caressed her a few more times.

Kyler was warm against him, with both her arms around his neck now as he controlled her, discovered her. Her soft moaning made his head pound and his temples throb. Her frame was so lean and slight it made him think of all the ways he could wield her body for his pleasure and hers. But he had to be patient! He drew on his years of study, his training in spells that took months to prepare. He wouldn't rush, not with her. She was hot inside, moist on his fingers. He suddenly withdrew and stood from the bed, wrenching his breeches down. He stepped out of them and returned to sit facing her. He tugged at the night gown, pulling it from her shoulders. Kyler helped him, pulling at the collar until it came free, and he slipped it off where it fell at her waist.

He pulled her into his arms, the orbs of her breasts pressed to his chest and the smooth skin of her back under his palms. He kissed her neck and throat, the long brown hair all over, draping her shoulders and falling on his arms. He found he was pulling it, guiding her head back to kiss her lips again. She received him, writhing and trembling against him with her sleek naked limbs. Leith's patience faded. He rocked her backwards, yanked her into position and climbed over her. Kyler's hands were on his chest and her legs opened for him. Her face was blushed and entranced, her hips arched slightly upwards.

He was engorged, with an almost painful pulsing in his loins. He kissed her once, twice . . . wait, he told himself. Go slow. He halted, nestling himself against her. She twitched when she felt him there, panting softly. He was on his elbows, caressing her face and waiting for her to be ready. He kissed her again, driving his tongue into her sweet, wanting mouth. Now, he thought. I'll take her now. Leith reached down to where their bodies met and orchestrated his entry. He pressed her— gently at first—then with more force until she whimpered and turned her head to one side.

"Don't be afraid," he said in her ear.

He pushed further, feeling the tender barrier begin to accept him. He was on fire, slowly penetrating, invading. He cursed his own magic, wishing it were strong enough in his lust to conjure a spell that would take her pain away. But, it came, he knew. Her flesh tore. She pitched in his arms and shrieked. He pinned her, using his weight to keep her still while he finished breaking her. She shut her eyes tight, letting out short sobs with each of his deliberate strokes. She endured him, bringing her hips to meet him though her face was wrecked with discomfort.

"That's it," he whispered.

He continued his cautious thrusts, her flesh so taut and narrow around him that he clenched his jaw from the pleasure. After a few moments, her body began to relent and her expression softened.

"Leith," she said, her arms reaching up and around his neck.

She was his, finally. For weeks he had stifled his desire, fighting it off every time she was near him. His nights were plagued with the image of her face, those noble eyes and supple, smiling lips always haunting him. In those moments he had found it hard to remember his dreary existence before this beautiful, rare creature appeared on his doorstep. Kyler's small, ink-stained fingers clawed at his shoulders as she lifted her head for another kiss. Leith gave it to her, pressing his mouth against her sighs.

In an instant, it broke upon him, more blissful and treacherous than any incantation he'd ever executed. Leith climaxed, rearing up and thrusting hard as she lay delicate and subdued as a flower beneath him. In his ecstasy, he heard her cry out again and clutch his forearm, her body yielding as he slowed his powerful movements. He lingered above her, caught his breath, and then lowered himself into her embrace. He slid his arms under her, resting his head on her shoulder. Her heartbeat murmured under his ear, and her skin was like silk against his cheek. Her fingers combed through his hair. His own pulse calmed in his veins, and the lantern's flame slowly flickered back to life.

Kyler opened her eyes to the morning. Slowly, she turned her head to find the empty, rumpled covers and the half-drawn bed curtain. Leith was gone. She threw back the covers, pulled on her robe and ventured upstairs. Kyler went to her cell, took up her brown robes and headed to the privy. She bathed at length, dried, and dressed. In the sanctuary of her room she cursed her will, curled onto the bed, and stared up at the window. Foolish girl! How had this treachery come to pass? The shame was an arrow in her chest. She had to speak to him, to restore what had surely been dismantled.

There was no one in the laboratory; the curtains were closed and the instruments were clean. There were no lessons on the table, no sign of him. Before long, she found herself on the stairs again, climbing upward until she stood outside her master's cracked door. She peered in, where she saw him staring down at an open book, a pair of black-rimmed spectacles resting on his nose. The witch was there, too, quietly writing something on a scroll in a corner. There was a bubbling noise, and a single lantern burned.

"You can linger out there all day if you wish," Leith's low voice resounded. Through the crack, he glanced up at her, pushing up his spectacles. "But you're welcome to come in."

Kyler stood a second more, then pushed the door open further. Her heart was racing. Leith wore his black velvet robes, his hands resting, palms flat, on either side of the book he studied. Marisele drew her red hood over her gauzy drape of hair, muttered disdainfully, and curled up over her scroll. The dragon's blood still boiled over the green fire, the bubbles coming slower than she'd seen last. It was thickening. Kyler stepped cautiously into the room, eyeing the books and baubles. She looked over at Marisele, then back at Leith, and chose her words carefully.

"I don't mean to intrude. I wanted to speak with you."

Leith pulled off his spectacles and surveyed her. A bite of tension shot down her spine, but she forced herself to meet his eyes. She felt herself blush at his piercing gaze, unable to read it. To her surprise, he smiled.

"I know you want to see it," he said, nodding at the beaker. Kyler looked over at it. "Go on."

He wasn't wrong—she was fascinated. She stepped nearer. It was beautiful to her, the languid bubbling and unnatural color. Kyler felt him approach over her shoulder.

"The glass is enchanted. Nothing else will hold it," he said. "And it won't break," he added, with an undertone of suspicion. "If it's spilled, it will drip to the ceiling and eat the roof through."

"How will it be done?" Kyler asked in a choked voice.

"I'll use it on the rocks beneath Malantheus' tomb. It will create an entryway. He is buried in a crypt, and the Hypnogoths prefer to roam the open. It is unlikely I will encounter one if I am quick and quiet."

"And the gauntlet?"

"I'll bring it here. A ritual must be performed."

Marisele leapt up from her scroll. "You seal your doom!" she told Leith. "The girl will flee with your plan at her ear and warn them. Don't you see?"

"I have no intention of attempting another escape," Kyler replied boldly. "The spirits have made it clear that I will not be leaving Solemn Woods any time soon."

"Don't patronize me, *scribe*," the witch snapped back. "Don't think I don't know how you've soiled my lord's concentration with your charms. He might have had the gauntlet in his grasp by now if not for you."

Kyler felt the blood rush to her face. She heard Leith's voice over her shoulder. "My apprentice is not responsible for our delay," he stated. "If anyone's concentration is soiled, it's yours. Perhaps you should take your project into your chamber where you'll be more at ease," he finished dryly.

Marisele stood, her frame hunched and her withered fists closed up like two dead roses. Grumbling to herself, she took up her things, then vanished behind the door, which she slammed shut.

Kyler jumped at the echoing boom, then sighed with relief. She turned. "Who is she, Leith? Where did she come from?"

There was a silence that gulped up the room.

"A village north of Storm Side. She was their seer until she failed to predict an attack of wolves that killed three children. After they took her eye as retribution, they sent her away. I imagine she took up with the Black Trade shortly after and eventually became a follower of Malantheus," he said.

Kyler blinked. "Malantheus? That's impossible. That would make her . . ."

"Hundreds of years old," he confirmed. "She was here when they cursed the woods, but not in human form. Marisele foresaw the Necromantis and quickly concealed herself in a tree to avoid damnation. There she remained, taking on its elements as the centuries passed. She aged as the tree aged, became dark, twisted, and gnarled with it," Leith told her, returning to the table. He looked up at a lantern on the hook above him. His brief stare lit it. "Weeks after I was exiled here she called to me. I freed her using this," he said, placing his hand on the book in front of him.

"The Grimoire," Kyler said gravely.

"I know you want a look," Leith said. Kyler kept her distance. "You are trapped here, Kyler," Leith reminded after her long hesitation. "You might as well busy yourself."

She dwelled on his words a moment, then moved toward the table as if the book were a dangerous animal she was bid to capture. It lay open to a sketch on one side, and the most beautiful black lettering she'd ever seen on the other. The drawing was of a skull, jaw open, a wreath of moonflower blossoms encircling it.

"The Reanimation Spell," Kyler read the symbols aloud.

"It's complicated," Leith said almost to himself, replacing his spectacles and running his fingers over the lettering. "My knowledge of the language is considerable, but not strong enough to translate the pages entirely," he said, his hand moving over to rest on a piece of parchment where a column of words was printed, some scratched out and scribbled over. "It's taken me months to research their meaning in the volumes I have in the library. Marisele is no help, either. It's been centuries since she was able to read it."

Kyler was silent, hypnotized by the elegant symbols of the Black Trade on the dried pages. Leith continued to file through his notes and scribbled another word on the parchment. He scratched his head. Kyler placed one hand on the table.

"I can," she admitted quietly.

"I know," he said. "But the Lunathyl symbols are very basic. Some of these I've never seen before."

"I mean, I can read it all," Kyler elaborated, taking up one of the pieces of parchment. "This one," she continued, pointing to one of his markings. "It isn't darkness, it's darken."

Leith stopped his work and stared at her. He took the parchment, compared it to a passage in the Grimoire and huffed. "Of course," he said. "How could you possibly . . .?"

"I had privileged sanction from all four Orders to study it," she explained. "I was commissioned to translate an exegesis written entirely in the language. I suppose once I began to learn some of the vocabulary, I was driven to learn it all. Since I was trusted to be alone in the restricted archives, well, I took advantage of my unique situation."

Kyler smiled up at him. Leith smiled back, but after a second it wilted. He took her by the arm and turned her to look at him levelly.

"You must know that what happens between us does not obligate you to abandon your convictions," he told her in a low tone. "I want things to be clear. I care for you. But I am going through with this."

Kyler felt her face flush again. "You must forgive me," she said. "If it was Wickham's purpose to use me as a distraction, I'm afraid I have become his pawn, after all. I am no seductress, my lord. I never meant to . . ."

"You have done me no disservice," Leith said, nearly laughing. "I never needed seducing. I wanted you." He reached up to gently stroke her chin. "Your own ideas of virtue and honor are what you battle with, and for that I can offer no assistance. Your will is your own when it comes to what part you wish to play in all of this."

Kyler pulled away and drifted across the room. "If your plot is executed there will be no black robes to earn, no stripes to strive for. What would I be if I returned now? A servant to the Chamber of Shadow only to invite them to use me again. What do I have to go back to?"

Leith gathered up the parchment and stacked it neatly next to the Grimoire. He pushed the book slightly toward her.

"If you would like to try your hand at it," he said, "I would be more than grateful."

Kyler turned. "You would trust me?"

"Perhaps I am unwise, but yes," he replied. "The kingdom can offer no one better suited, I fear. That, and I know you are itching for it," he said, lifting an eyebrow. "Of course, this will give you every opportunity to sabotage my efforts, but I suppose a betrayal is due me. Nythos surely has his punishment ready."

"If I help you, innocent people will die," Kyler said.

"That may be. But, perhaps not. It will likely be soldiers, no more than the Academy is already willing to sacrifice in any battle. I intend to give an opportunity for surrender, of course," said Leith. "It may be easier to spare lives with your influence."

"How?"

"I am not held in high regard. One so known for her loyalty to the Academy may be able to make a case for the cause."

Kyler paused in thought. She wondered if it was possible. What would be left for her after his victory if she escaped him? What would become of her if she was able to stop him? Leith would likely be executed, and she would never earn her robes for the forbidden spells she had learned, even if she could convince them she did so under his power. In this, she had a purpose. The Academy could never toss her to the side again. She had never felt her worth more strongly than she did now.

"I am left with few other options," she said. "You've proven your faith in me. I want to return the favor."

There was an earnest mark in his eyes, then, something like remorse. Leith nodded to himself, stepped away from the table and gestured for her to come to it. Kyler took his place and began to work. She sensed him loitering behind her, watching. Then, his tall shadow moved across the walls against the firelight until she heard the creak of his chamber door as he eased it half-closed. Her gaze danced over the ancient letters, and the quill marked forbidden words on the parchment. Something inside her had come alive.

Kyler's eyes shot open wide. It was the third time she had nodded off. Her mind spun with symbols and words—*Awake, these souls take breath once more. The curved line over a half-moon. Darken your desire, become . . . what is it? Over a half moon . . . revenge.* Yes, that's it. Kyler's eyes drooped. She dipped the quill, but the ink well was empty. *Become revenge.* She shivered, closed her eyes and breathed in deeply. Kyler put down the quill and rubbed her face with her hands. She exhaled. The parchment was complete. There was the trace of a grin on her mouth—criminal, satisfied. She turned toward Leith's chamber.

His room was dark, of course, some light pouring in as she pushed open his door. His shadow lurked at the giant form of the desk, the cobalt glimmer of his eyes only slightly illuminating a stack of books in front of him. She stood in the doorway a moment, holding the parchment loosely at her side, her other hand on the frame. An unused candle sparked to life on the nightstand next to his unmade bed. Kyler eyed it, then glanced back over to see Leith turning from his work to face her.

"I'm sorry," she said.

"Don't be."

Kyler paused. "I've finished."

"Let me see," Leith said.

She brought it to him, feeling uneasy coming further into his chamber. He took it, looking it over with a great deal of delight, something she'd never seen him express. As he did, she gazed over at the bed, the gray sheets and dark blanket tousled and twisted. Kyler's mind was roused, recalling his body over her, his shoulders like wide, rugged crags, and his beautiful eyes storming down into hers. Leith broke her trance by touching her hand. He took it in his, and she instinctively squeezed as he brought it to his lips.

"You're extraordinary," he said in a whisper.

Kyler's heart pounded, and heat raced to her limbs and face as he held her hand in his own, his touch already intimate, as if he'd been her lover for ages. But, the doubt and confusion overcame her. She wondered what he truly felt for her. Regardless of how vehemently she admired and craved him, Kyler couldn't help the dreadful feeling that all she had done was make herself another one of his whores.

"I'm also very tired," she answered weakly.

"Lie down if you wish," he offered, nodding at his bed.

She winced at the words, her eyes flicking over to the bed and trying to form a reply. It was strangely inviting to her, the dark corner, the canopy, and the heavy curtain. The room was saturated with his scent and the bed posts were accented with incense burners. Imagining her head on his soft pillow was making her even drowsier. She didn't want to voice the obvious. She didn't want to ask where he would sleep if she took the bed.

"You don't mind?"

"No," he answered simply, and let her hand go.

"Thank you," Kyler said, and headed toward the bed.

She climbed up onto the covers, rested her head on the pillow, and tucked her hands under her neck. The bed was worn and soft, and smelled of sandalwood. Kyler let her eyes close, and the sound of Leith's chair creaking as he turned pages lulled her to sleep.

The night once more offered her the most peculiar of visions. The drawing of the skull and the glowing rune stones invaded, but there were no nightmares. Her mind ventured outside the walls of the old observatory. Salyndria's landscape was vast before her, the jagged gray mountains of the West, the clouds over Storm Side. The long, hollow tunnel of Black Burrow, where the Pithfolk live, was vivid in her dreams. Kyler tossed in her sleep. There were the vales of the East, the Chamber of Spirit, shadowy and magnificent on Ash Plain. Somewhere in a cave, a fire burned. A pile of weapons and belongings sat in a corner, and Kyler looked up from the flames as Leith entered and pulled off his snow-flecked hood.

Kyler woke on her side. He was behind her in the darkness, his hands prying and his breath heavy. Leith's body pressed hers, his fingers searching and feeling under her brown robes, his silver rings cold on her skin. She rolled over toward him, but she could see nothing. No candle burned, no lantern gave light. This was what he wanted. She drowsily reached up and searched for him, finding his bare, muscled arms, then his neck and face. He kissed her, impatiently tugging up the robes until she was exposed. He touched her there cautiously, lightly, and she squirmed and convulsed until she was moist again. He pulled her farther down the bed, then suddenly his lips were on her stomach, his hands gripping her hips.

Kyler looked up at the dark ceiling. She grappled at the covers, waiting. His mouth reached her, his tongue hot and insistent between her legs. Her mouth gaped open at the sudden pleasure, her hips coursing upward in his grip. She moaned loudly, tugging a fistful of the covers. His tongue was like fire, fluidly dancing over her flesh again and again, baiting and teasing her. He pressed his tongue inside against the tender, wounded brim, and with gentle, heedful movements, he brought her toward ecstasy once more.

"Leith!" Kyler cried, her body tensed and ready.

He served her with more rapid flicks and suckling kisses, his fingers digging into her hips. She opened her legs wider, reaching between them to feel for the black locks of his hair. The spike of pleasure rose up, and Kyler nursed it desperately. She groaned as it took her over, arching her back and stretching her arms over her head to clutch the pillow when it finally came. She rocked back and forth against his mouth, milking all that was left of her climax from him. Slowly, she relaxed, her body shaking in his hands. She shyly brought her thighs together as he raised his head.

Leith's hands roamed her thighs inquisitively, navigating up to her hips and then her waist. The tips of his fingers played there, tracing around her navel and under her ribs. He was a seated shadow before her, his face obscured by the darkness and his silhouette almost unmoving. Then, with a match of force and regard, he took hold of her body and turned her on her stomach. Kyler yipped fretfully and tried to crawl away, but he seized her.

"Don't," he commanded, his body like a cage over her. "I won't hurt you."

He brushed her hair aside, then pressed his lips and tongue to her shoulder and the nape of her neck. Her eyes closed and she surrendered, as if stunned by a venomous predator. His knee came up under her leg and bent it into position. He slid her robes up past her hips and pulled her to him. Kyler trembled as he entered her, the torn flesh stretching and stinging. She let out a worried, bird-like chirp, to which Leith replied by slowing his rhythm and lowering himself to her ear.

"It will be all right," he whispered softly.

And it was. Kyler relished him, thick and solid inside her as the pain subsided and was replaced by his fullness rubbing against the parts of her body he'd awakened. Engulfed in darkness, he made love to her, his body heavy and exacting, his erection sliding smoothly in and out of her. He grunted over her shoulder, his strokes becoming faster and more forceful. His arms were like stone pillars on either side of her, and she reached out to snare one when she sensed he was nearly finished. His muscles were hard under her fingers. She curved her back, bringing her haunches up to counter his thrusts. That was all it took.

Leith shouted, got to his knees and took her hips in his hands. His body pulsed with the last few strokes, and his grip slowly relaxed. Soon they were both limp and exhausted, lying next to each other on the tangled covers.

CHAPTER EIGHT

THE GAUNTLET

Dawn prowled in through the windows. Leith's shuffling woke his apprentice. She was nude under the covers, lifting her head from the pillow to look at him in the stifled amethyst light. She sat up in the bed, clutching the covers to her, and flicked a hand at the candle by the bed. The small flame she rendered made him turn. He was dressing and gathering tools into a pack.

"You're going after it," she said.

"They will be resting at this hour," Leith answered. He continued dressing, pulling on a black cloak and stepping into thick boots. "I was hoping to be gone when you woke."

"Why?" she asked.

"So you couldn't ask to come along," he said, buttoning up.

"And if I do?"

Leith sighed and rubbed his eyes. "I would tell you it will be dangerous, that if they hear us we could be killed or captured. I would tell you that if my plan fails and I am punished, that you would be punished with me."

"And if I still wish to come?"

Leith looked over at her with a slanted smile. He came to sit on the bed. "I would know that even if I forbid it, you would follow me to Lamentiose, anyway. You are as willful as you are beautiful."

"You don't think I would have worked to uncover Malantheus' secrets just to lounge here while you make history, do you?" she said, leaning toward his ear. "Besides, perhaps the gods sent me here for a reason. Maybe I am meant to play a part in what you are about to do."

Leith reached up to sweep a lock of hair from her forehead. "I would hate to be in a position," he said, "where I am absent your expertise."

Kyler smirked and lifted her chin. "Then it's settled," she said.

The tunnel was damp and dark. Kyler carried a lantern, Leith leading the way past the plumeroot and the watered rock. They reached the open chamber where the Lunathyl marked their destination. Kyler set the lantern down and helped him slide the platform aside. Leith reached into his pack and pulled out the bottle of dragon's blood. It was fixed with a stopper, the liquid resting at the top, the bottom empty. Leith motioned for Kyler to stand back. He turned the bottle upside down. Once the blood slumped to the bottom, he pulled out the stopper. He gave Kyler a look.

"Remember," he told her in a whisper, "keep a sharp eye, and no magic. Any spells will attract the Hypnogoths. Stay close to me."

She nodded. With that, Leith turned the bottle. The fluid slid up and out, thick crimson droplets rising from the rim to the roof. Instantly it went to work, hissing and smoking as it struck the rock overhead. The dragon's blood continued to rise from the bottle, the hissing growing louder as more droplets joined the red pool as it fumed and sizzled. Soon, a speck of silvery light broke through the ceiling. It spread and grew bright as the blood consumed the rock, a hole opening and widening out to meet the Lunathyl where it finally waned to form an edge.

The hissing ceased, and the smoke faded at the borders of the opening. Leith's bottle was empty. Through the hole above, torches could be seen atop short, white pillars that lined a circular vault. The fire that burned in them was a pale, glittering silver, a ball-shaped flame that hovered over shallow metal vessels. Leith eyed the hole with scrutiny, then nodded at Kyler. She picked up the lantern and extinguished it, then helped him return the platform to the center of the room. Leith climbed it and lifted himself through. Kyler followed, and he pulled her up.

They stood in an ante chamber, its round, white walls marked with runes and trimmed with niches where skulls were placed. A tall door flanked by two dragon statues with spears in their claws faced them. Behind was another door, bound by heavy locks and bolts that glowed red.

"That one leads out. It's enchanted," he said, then approached the door where the statues sat. He stared at it. Kyler waited behind him. Leith's blue eyes narrowed into slits and he rubbed his chin as he looked at the statues. "Guarded by beasts in arms that never sleep," he said.

"Yes," Kyler said excitedly. "From *The History of the Nefarious Gauntlet*. Beasts in arms whose weapons keep . . ." she added, her brow knitted with concentration, "whose weapons keep, sealed by lance, unlocked by grace." Suddenly, she looked up at the runes. "It's here," she said, pointing. "Unlocked by grace and circumstance."

Her exhilaration dimmed, and she frowned as Leith approached. "What is that supposed to mean? And what are those for?" she asked, pointing up at two empty brackets on either side of the paragraph of runes.

Leith reached up to touch one. They were silver plates affixed with protruding braces. He looked back at her. They traded a look of realization and returned to the statues. "The spears," said Leith. "The spears must be removable."

He gripped one and pulled, but it wouldn't budge. He pulled on the other one, using all his strength, but it didn't move, either. Leith huffed, then began to pace the room with his hands on his hips. Kyler tilted her head as she looked at them.

"Perhaps they must both be pulled at once."

Leith blinked and stared. His hands dropped. He approached the statues again and motioned to Kyler. She took hold of the left spear and he took hold of the right. Together they yanked, and the spears finally came loose, sliding from the dragons' claws until they each held one. They waited, but the door didn't open.

"The gods must be playing a joke on us," Kyler remarked.

"No," Leith said, taking his spear over to the silver brackets. "Not this time," he said, and slipped the lance into the brace.

The torches sparked. He beckoned for Kyler. She brought hers to the other side and placed it into the second brace. Instantly, something commenced somewhere behind the walls, a mechanism coming to life, a rumbling of stone against stone. The door eased open, revealing a short staircase leading up.

"Aren't you glad I came along?" she asked.

The stairs spiraled. Malantheus's crypt was at the top of a tower, a four-cornered room with windows barred by iron grating in a pattern of winding, thorny vines. Morning light struck cavities in the decorated walls where skeletons were laid, the clothes they wore in life still clinging in scraps to their bones. The view of Lamentiose was partially obscured by the windows' grid—a vast, misted moor flecked with hundreds of crumbling headstones and marked here and there by larger mausoleums.

"I can hear the ocean," she whispered as they entered. "Leith, look," she said, peering out the window and down at the ground where several skeletons lay at the foot of the tower, their clothes and armor of more modern fashion still intact.

"They tried to climb up," Leith told her. "The tower is equipped with retracting spikes. Any extra weight on the stones will trigger them. Come away from the windows," he warned, and they both stepped into the center of the room.

Malantheus's tomb was before them, a heavy, rectangular vault standing four feet high and topped with a jagged stone cover on a round platform, which was ringed with ancient markings. It was made of black and gray marble, with smooth miniature pillars running up its four corners. The top was accented by the stone likeness of a Kithra, a small winged and horned creature said to guard wicked souls from resurrection. Leith and Kyler advanced toward it carefully. The pale, purple dawn streaked in through the windows onto the tomb. Kyler reached out to touch it.

"So quiet," she whispered, with a tone of alarm. "And cold."

"We must try to open it together," Leith said, stepping up onto the platform. "If I slide it, it will be too loud. See if you can lift it."

Kyler joined him, gripping the jagged sides of the marble top, and inadvertently looking into the steadfast ruby eyes of the Kithra. She swallowed a lump in her throat and heaved. The top swayed then lifted, and they carefully brought it to rest on the ground beside the tomb. Kyler caught her breath and glanced up at Leith over the statue. They exchanged a glance, snatching one last look at each other in somber anticipation, as they were both about to alter the world they knew. They returned to the tomb.

The corpse of Malantheus lay in shadow, the gray bones covered in weathered armor and wilted black velvet. His hooded skull tilted to one side, the jaw open with crooked, broken teeth. It didn't seem he was even a tall or large man, his stone-colored skeleton taking up not even the length of the coffin. The armor was unique, likely pieced together and created by the Black Trade just for him. There was a large breastplate over his rib cage, inlaid with black stone panels and runes on the shoulders. His fingernails were long and tapered, and his grey hair curled to his collarbone and decorated his skull like dried moss. There was no headpiece, no jewelry. It seemed he was to be buried without such honor, left only with the symbols of the Black Trade to decay with him.

Kyler breathed out with shock and excitement. They both shared a grin like two children up to mischief. "Look at him," she whispered.

Malantheus' arms were crossed at his chest. He wore no gauntlet. Over his abdomen, there was only a rectangular box, made of the same marble as the tomb and etched with silver stars and moons. It was bolted by thick silver bands and decorated on top by a round impression.

"There it is," Leith said on a warm breath, his sharp, blue eyes fixed on the box with awe.

He took it slowly from the darkness of the tomb and brought it to the floor. They both kneeled to examine it further. Leith ran his fingers over the smooth silver latches, turning the box over in his hands. He studied it severely, his focus finally resting on the impression on the lid.

"It's a lock," he said with a clenched jaw. "It needs a key."

With that, he rose and stiffly paced the room. He cursed quietly, then came to stand at the top of the staircase, motionless and deep in thought. Kyler's brow wrinkled once more at her master's frustration. She turned to the box, looking it over again. She placed her fingers over the lock, touching the circular impression, finding the grooves and oval-shaped pits. Suddenly, she let out a sharp gasp, nearly choking on her own breath. She clapped her hand over her mouth and recoiled from the box.

"What is it?" Leith asked, returning to her.

"It couldn't be!"

"Shhh!" he warned, dropping to his knees to calm her. "What is it?"

Kyler quickly removed her amulet. Her hands trembled as she fit the charm over the lock, gems faced downward, and watched it drop perfectly into place. They were both quiet as death, and she struggled to keep her fingers still as she turned it clockwise. The only sound was the distant crashing of waves and the click of the latches as they came loose.

"Nythos, be merciful!" she whispered. "How can this be?"

"Unlocked by grace," Leith recited, his bewildered expression coming to rest on Kyler. "And circumstance. How did you know?" he asked her, his face marked with suspicion.

"I've worn it since I was a child," she defended. "I've run my hand over it a thousand times. The impression is identical." When Leith's distrusting expression did not waver, she stood up from the box. "You dare doubt my honor now?"

"It's difficult to understand," he told her as he rose to his feet, "how this could come to pass, that you happen to be with me now at this moment."

"The words are centuries old!" she told him, pointing down the steps toward the antechamber where the runes were carved. "I don't know how I came to be here, either. Stop looking at me as if I've any knowledge of this!"

What interrupted them, then, was a sound so unsettling that the morning seemed to hush and the sun might as well have hidden itself away. There was a vicious, terrible howling, a dissonant scream that pierced the peaceful dawn. Leith and Kyler looked at each other now with immediate panic. He rushed over to the windows, gazing down into the lifting mist from where the headstones peeked out. The dark figures were moving quickly, contorted limbs jerking as they advanced on all fours among the graves. There were two, then four, then five—all of them moving in a determined, deadly clamber toward the tower. Their saffron eyes were glowing points in the gray fog.

Leith whirled around and sank back to the ground. He tossed Kyler her amulet and tucked the box under his arm. "Run!" he commanded, and they raced for the staircase.

Leaping over every step, they flew until the silver light greeted them once more. The peculiar balls of firelight were sparking madly as the Hypnogoths' terrible screeching grew loud and close. The red glow of the bolts on the door leading outside had vanished, and the sound of locks clicking and chains rattling echoed. Leith gripped Kyler's arm with his free hand as the Hypnogoths breached the door. Kyler sucked in a breath as one appeared on the threshold, a wasted figure with wrinkled, indigo skin and three gangly fingers as long as a wand wrapped around the latch. Its yellow eyes were fixed on the box under Leith's arm. The hollow, lipless mouth opened with a shrill cry of protest.

"Jump!" Leith yelled, and they rushed the hole in the floor where they toppled onto the platform, then jumped down to the ground.

Leith took Kyler's wrist and pulled. They broke into a run out of the chamber and into the narrow tunnel. Shadows crossed the light as the Hypnogoths climbed down into the hole. Kyler glanced back. They moved fast, like anxious spiders after an insect got tangled in their web, their dark silhouettes scrambling after her.

"Don't look back!" Leith ordered, tugging on her wrist.

They ran as fast as they could, the torches blustering as they passed. The creatures howled in their chase, the beating of their feet and hands on the rock growing closer. They were gaining. Kyler's lungs burned as she struggled to keep up with Leith, her boots like boulders and her wrist chafed by his determined grip. The conduit came into view, and Leith sprinted toward it. Kyler lost her pace and tripped suddenly over a large root, only a few feet from the runes.

"Leith!" she cried.

He was already on his knees beside her, and they both realized her boot was stuck under the root. He pulled at it frantically, but it wouldn't come loose. His eyes flicked up at their pursuers, then at several large rocks that dotted the floor and roof of the tunnel. He clenched his jaw. He needed time.

"Leave me!" Kyler told him. "You have the gauntlet. It's you they're after."

"They'll punish you with madness," he said. "They'll take over your mind. Congregum Obstruco!" he shouted, and raised his hand at the rocks.

Instantly, they obeyed him, each one lifting from its ledge and rapidly assembling before them to form a wall. The last one fell in place as the Hypnogoths reached the barricade, their shrill voices making Kyler jump as they reached their long arms through the gaps in the rock and groped for her.

"Leith!" she cried, as one rigid, purple hand swiped at her. "Flame!" she shouted, raising her palm at the creature.

The fire leapt from her hand in a burst of heat, causing the Hypnogoth to scream and recoil.

Leith gripped the root that held her shoe. "Fracturo!" he commanded.

The thick root snapped in his hand and he yanked several times, grunting as it finally came free. Kyler slipped her foot out and stumbled toward the conduit. Leith ushered her up onto the slab and wrapped an arm around her, but she squealed suddenly with dismay. One of the Hypnogoths had seized her by the ankle, its devious eyes peeking at her through the rocks. They had pulled one loose, providing a large enough breach to stretch one long arm inside.

"Take us back!" Kyler pleaded.

"I can't! I'll bring it with us!" Leith told her. Kyler looked into its eyes, those tiny black spots quickly entrancing her. She relaxed in Leith's hold, suddenly staring at the creature as if it were a beautiful painting. She stopped resisting, and Leith felt her being pulled from him. "Kyler, look away," he said gravely. "Look away! *Dismantium!*" he told the rocks, and the barricade collapsed.

Their shrieks pierced his ears, but the Hypnogoth had released her. Leith pulled her close. In an instant, they both disappeared in a cloud of dust.

The morning sun streamed into the hollow dome as Leith and Kyler reappeared, huddled together on the platform. Kyler coughed from the dust and clung to him. Leith clutched her tightly with one arm. The other held the marble box with as much force.

"We're safe," he told her, his lips next to her ear. "It's all right."

"We're doomed," she said mournfully, and pushed herself out to face him. "How will the gods ever forgive us?"

"The gods gave up on me long ago," he answered. "It's time I returned their indifference. Come," he said, as he rose and pulled her with him.

Leith shoved aside the scrolls and books, placing the gauntlet's box on his desk in the study. Kyler hovered, waiting. He pulled on the latch and lifted the lid. With a faint creak of hinges and the flash of silver against a candle flame, the famed relic was revealed. It resembled the armored gloves of Salyndria's soldiers: thick, smooth steel with scrollwork on the edges of the plating. The tarnished chain mail fingers were capped by smooth, metal links and a bronze knuckle plate with rounded, beveled ends. The metal still had its sheen after so many years, and it reflected the saffron firelight in the room. The sleeve came to a tapered end past the wrist, where it ended in a triangle of bronze. This was the weapon that caused so much suffering. The passionate work of Malantheus's followers could be seen in its detailed carvings: symbols were artfully etched on the back of the hand to form a word in the Black Trade.

"Dominion," Kyler read aloud. "It looks so . . ."

"Ordinary," Leith finished, with a shred of disappointment in his voice.

"Turn it over," Marisele's squeak interrupted.

They both looked back. She had emerged from her cell, likely having sensed their return. She was alert, hobbling quickly over on her cane. Leith gingerly took the gauntlet from the box. It was heavy in his hands, the metal cold on his fingers and the steel reflecting his eyes. He was smiling with childlike delight. He admired its craftsmanship, tracing the ancient etching and scrollwork with fascination. It was finally in his grasp! Leith turned it over to expose the underside of the glove. There, in the candlelight, were four short spikes on the inside of the sleeve. The tips were tinted dark red.

"Yes," Marisele hissed, pointing as she approached the table.

"What are those?" Kyler asked.

"The gauntlet needs the blood of its master to function. They become one," she explained with a lunacy in her wide eye.

Marisele stared intently at the glove, grinning wildly. The witch reached out. Leith quickly placed the gauntlet in the box and shut the lid. Marisele frowned and her hand snaked back.

"We will perform the ritual tonight," he said.

"Tonight! Don't you see how much time we've wasted already?" she barked, stamping her cane on the floor.

"There is more work to be done," Leith countered. "Tonight," he repeated decisively, taking the box under his arm once more. "Be sure your ingredients are prepared," he told Marisele.

She glowered at him, her lips pursed. After a moment, she disarmed and smiled. "Of course," she said on the end of a cough, and backed away.

Kyler poured over the scrolls once more while sipping a hot drink made from Leith's stores of powdered ginger and pumpkin. She sat at the smaller desk in Leith's chamber, the marble box not far from her on the nightstand. The parchment was neatly arranged, the incantations in order, and all the passages translated in her spruce script. She pulled a drape of brown hair over one shoulder like a scarf then looked over at Leith. He sat back, massaging his arm. He had landed hard on it when they jumped through the opening in the crypt.

"Are you all right?" Kyler asked him, taking another sip.

Leith grunted and stood from the chair. He pulled off his robes and slung them over it, leaving himself bare-chested in only his trousers. He examined his muscled upper arm, finding a colorful bruise. Kyler turned all the way around in her chair. He crossed the room to his bed, where he climbed up and onto his back. Kyler stood.

She came toward the bed and shed her robes to the linen frock she wore under it. Leith opened his arms for her as she crawled in next to him. He rested his chin on the top of her head and she settled her cheek onto his collarbone, one hand curving around his neck. Leith stroked her hair, feeling her leg curl around his.

"I'm sorry I doubted you," he told her. "At the crypt." Kyler answered with the gentle movements of her body, her limbs wrapping around him like climbing vines. "I fear there are forces much greater than ours at work," he said. "You and I were not tossed together in this plight by accident."

Soon, her mouth was covering his neck in light kisses, and her thighs were languidly rubbing against his. Kyler raised herself up and climbed on top of him. He reached up for her face and rose to kiss her, but she coyly drew back with a mischievous smile. His excitement mounted, and he countered by catching her hips and centering her over his growing erection.

"You feel that?" he whispered up at her.

"Yes," she breathed, her poise shattered as she started to tremble again.

He guided her hips back and forth over it. Kyler's eyes closed and her head fell back. She pulled the frock from her shoulders and let it drop, revealing her soft, perfect breasts. He touched them, heavy teardrops in his hands, the peaks pink and firm under his palms. His face felt hot as he took in the spectacle of her naked body above him: the smooth, level plain of her stomach as it vanished under the cloth fallen at her waist, the long spiraling hair cascading over her slender frame. She grew bold again, her fingers trying to work at the ties on his pants. He quickly assisted her, pushing them down and kicking them off as if they were shackles, before placing her right back where she was.

"Slowly," he told her as she reached down for him. "There."

She was slick on his crown, her warm flesh and inexperience teasing him. She was blushing, clumsy at her task until finally she ushered him inside. He took her waist in his grip and bore deeper, delighting in the sensual movements and sounds she made in response. Leith instructed her with his hands, training her in the rhythm, then releasing her to move as it pleased her. How quickly she learned! Already, she was bringing herself to climax. Her sighs and moans grew louder and more urgent as she moved like a snake on top of him, her abdomen undulating, the muscles tensing. She convulsed as her pleasure came, her head rolling back again. With all his willpower he resisted thrusting, allowing her the control until she was spent and fulfilled.

Then, he rose up to meet her, her breasts paradise in his mouth, her backside firm and smooth in his grasp. He took over the pace where it had ebbed, eager to have his turn at using her body for his satisfaction. He kneaded her with his sex, bringing her to him over and over like waves to a cliff. He seized the back of her neck and kissed her. Under her muffled, contented murmurs he found his orgasm, parting from her lips to let out several groans as he stroked her twice, three times more. Her skin was wet with sweat, that sweet, faint perfume mingling with a woman's scent. Leith held her to him, kissing her temple between heavy breaths.

"You've taught me so much more than magic," Kyler whispered.

CHAPTER NINE
THE RITUAL

When twilight came, Leith and Kyler joined Marisele in the study. They had cleared out a space in the center of the room, where they placed a table. Marisele mixed the potion, her ground powders and thick liquids already prepared. Kyler laid out the Grimoire and the scrolls she'd completed. Marisele poured a circle of bat blood on the table while Leith took the gauntlet carefully from the box and placed it in the middle. The gold light outside gave way to evening shadows. Something stirred in the woods, and a wicked wind roamed the thick, haggard trees. As Leith spoke the first words, it seemed an unknown force slowed the setting sun. The ritual began.

The soldier's massive, armored chest rattled with laughter at the words on the ancient oak. The company joined him, except for two, who traded grave looks. Rowan eyed his only colleague: a young woman from the Order of Spirit, her purple robe cluttered with gold charms and gem pendants, the smooth, dark skin of her face tattooed at the temples with archaic symbols. Her great black horse snorted as a light snow fell.

"What do you sense, Azrani?" he asked her.

The woman threw back her hood, revealing black hair cut close to her scalp in tiny curls.

"As I've said," she told him in a low voice, "this is a terrible idea."

"What are we waiting for?" one of the four soldiers growled as he urged his horse toward the darkness of Solemn Woods with a hard kick. "To let the girl make your decisions? Come! My sword wants a stain!"

"You promised us gold, seer," another, older one said to Rowan through the gaps in his dented helmet. "Let's not be idle. I've made this Leith bleed before and I won't miss a second helping. Let the spirits leer at us like orphans at rich men. The girl lets fear guide her."

"I let prudence guide me," Azrani countered sharply. "Evil stirs beyond those trees," she said, then stopped, perked, and looked up. A hard wind came rushing through, sweeping up the snow and tossing it. "And something else," she added, her black eyes narrowing into slits as she pulled her hood back up.

"I want what I was promised," the soldier reminded them, the others grunting in agreement.

Rowan gulped, then looked fretfully at the trail in front of them. He nodded, then advanced ahead of the crowd. They followed.

The twilight lingered unnaturally long outside the windows. The study began to smell of blood and ashes as Leith neared the end of the incantation. Kyler turned his pages, his hoarse voice roaring out the words as the gauntlet began to spark before him. Kyler jumped back, but Leith remained inert. Marisele stood patiently by, watching the gauntlet with a wide, eager eye.

"Awake! These souls take breath once more. Darken your desire. Become revenge!" Leith thundered. As he spoke, the word etched in the steel began to glow like embers. "The potion," he told Marisele.

She limped forward and held out a vial. Leith poured a blue liquid slowly over the runes. It streamed down in a peculiar way, never touching the table but instead coating the entire hand piece, sizzling as it covered the word. Then the liquid retreated, as if sucked up by the etching itself—but the etching had changed. As the last of the potion disappeared, another set of runes revealed itself in a luminescent sapphire color. The runes formed a secret spell, one neither he nor Kyler had ever seen in any book. They looked at each other. Leith tuned back to the gauntlet and read the runes aloud.

"Rise, death and demise," he said.

At once, the gauntlet sparked again, this time engulfed by jagged forks that looked like lightning. Leith stepped back as it began to transform, sharp spikes appearing on the knuckles where the rays struck, the steel shifting into jagged edges, and the fingers tapering into points. At last it settled, the metal retaining a charged, sapphire brilliance. Leith smiled with satisfaction.

"It's so unfortunate," Marisele squeaked, as Leith and Kyler came close to the table. They ignored her, staring at the glove with awe.

"You did it," Kyler said to him.

"So unfortunate," the old woman said again.

They looked up at her. "What is, Marisele?" Leith finally responded.

"All that work—and you won't be able to wear it," she snarled, suddenly taking her withered hands from her sleeves and clapping them together. "I had hoped you and I would share this victory. But it seems you've chosen your little whore over the woman who has been by your side from the beginning!" Before either of them could react, the old witch had gathered a spell to her in a bright ball of light. "Trucido!" she squealed, then released it at Leith.

It threw him back against the wall. He fell to the ground in a heap of black velvet, blood trickling from his ears.

"Leith!" Kyler screamed in terror, as she threw herself over him. "Leith!" she said again, shaking him and watching for his closed eyes to open. His skin had gone instantly pale, the color drained from his lips. A crater of burnt cloth was visible on his robe at the chest. He wasn't breathing. Kyler felt tears sting her cheeks, and a rage she'd never felt before grew hot in her blood.

"Such a clever sorcerer!" Marisele cackled as she approached the table and took up the glowing gauntlet. "Such a shame."

The witch fitted the glove over her shriveled arm, then began to flinch violently as the spikes pierced her flesh. Marisele cried out as blood dripped down her arm onto the sleeve of her red robe, then grinned menacingly as she admired her new accessory. Kyler clutched Leith's robes, then checked his face again. His chest was still. His eyes remained closed.

"Treacherous crone!" Kyler wailed as she brought herself to her feet. "I'll kill you for this!" she shrieked fiercely, her fist balled and her magic ready.

"Not likely," Marisele croaked, then aimed the gauntlet at her. "The plan was ours. His and mine! All these years here in this place together, and you've destroyed everything. We were going to rule Salyndria. But he made his choice, a man blinded by flesh. Perhaps the afterlife will show him what a mistake he made."

The lightning forks sparked again and gathered at the pointed fingertips. The electric streams snaked out at Kyler, but she dodged them and threw herself to the ground. The wall behind her bore a charred crater where before there was stone. Quickly, Kyler raced for the door, the sound of Marisele's spell striking more spots on the wall and echoing close as Kyler reached the stairway. The witch's frustrated screeches followed, her cane thumping loudly on the stairs as she struggled to chase Kyler. The darkening cylinder lit up bright as morning as Marisele tried again. Kyler darted skillfully up toward the dome, escaping the lightning streams as they burned another crater in the stone.

When Marisele reached the vacant room, it was already too late. There was a cloud of metallic dust settling over the conduit. The bats stirred above her, angry at the gauntlet's light. The old witch leaned on her cane and laughed loudly.

"Let the Hypnogoths have you, slut!" she proclaimed as she turned on her heel.

Meanwhile, Rowan and his company were deep in the forest, the clink of metal shields against swords and the determined hoof beats of the horses the only sounds in the dusk. At the onset, the soldiers had been cautious and ready, eyeing the misted trees with weapons at their fingertips. As the dark trail wore on, however, the spirits failed to show themselves, and the company's discretion grew lax. Even the howling wind that gave Solemn Woods its famous whisper was silent.

"What legendary wickedness!" one of the soldiers mocked.

"I, for one, am thoroughly terrified," said another with sharp sarcasm.

The four of them laughed, mock-haunting each other with loud wailing as the horses kept a steady pace. Rowan and Azrani maintained a stride behind. The forest was empty, barren.

"I don't understand," Rowan remarked to his friend. "Don't you sense anything?"

"I can't explain it," Azrani said. "There are no spirits here. I sense no presence but the living. But the stillness," she added, looking to her right and left, "it's like a drawing-back." With that she stopped her horse and stared straight ahead at the trail. "Like water from a shoreline before a mighty wave. Something waits, Rowan. Something is coming."

Just then, another voice joined the soldiers' taunts. It echoed in every direction, making it impossible to find its source. It was a shrill, piercing call, a human voice shouting out over the woods. The company stopped to listen.

"By our gods, what is that?" one of them said.

There was wicked laughter, followed by a stream of what sounded like commands, the words like dissonant notes of blaring music that rung out through the thicket of warped branches. There was a faint light ahead to the right of the snow-laden trail—a flickering, sparking beam. Then there was the movement of shadows in the trees. All around them, the cold, misted ground erupted with small holes. To their horror, they watched as skeletal hands emerged. Corpses climbed up from the snow. Sallow, vein-flecked skin, dirt-crusted hair, and torn clothing returned to the bones in front of their eyes. The bodies grew robes and pale flesh, like dead plants recovering leaves.

From behind the gnarled sable trunks of the trees, more approached. As faces formed rapidly over ashen skulls, their mouths grinned and their eyes without irises shone like frosted windows. There were four, then six, then seven. Close to a dozen men and women wearing robes of all colors advanced slowly toward them. The soldiers' horses bucked and whinnied in dismay.

"How can it be?" Azrani exclaimed. "They live! That's why I could not sense them. Turn back, I beseech all of you!"

"They are ghosts," one of the soldiers countered, pulling his sword from its sheath. "And notorious for fooling the eye. Surely a sorceress of your Order should see," he mocked, as the corpses drew slowly closer.

"These are not spirits—they are as alive as you and me," Azrani assured. She cautiously urged her horse to retreat as she clutched a charm at her neck. "Forgive me, Rowan, but these woods house an ancient vengeance I cannot combat. May the gods be merciful!" she added, before turning her horse and quickly fleeing.

The soldiers laughed at her departure. Rowan watched fearfully as Azrani's figure vanished into the mist.

"She is highly decorated," he defended weakly. Images suddenly flashed before him—broken shields in the snow, and a small dark pit where toadstools grew. "Perhaps she speaks the truth."

"I'll show you the truth," said the soldier who held the sword, before giving it a determined thrust at a young male in a red robe who approached his horse.

The sword ran him through and stuck, dark syrup oozing from the boy's chest and mouth. The boy looked down at his injury with curiosity. Rowan was frozen with horror. Never in Salyndria's vast history had anyone made a specter bleed. Azrani was right. The corpse-boy's pearled eyes shifted up at the soldier, who was staring blankly and still gripping the hilt of his sword. The boy smirked, his teeth saturated with the dark blood, and reached up. He yanked the huge, armored soldier from his horse, making him fall, bewildered, onto his back.

The boy gripped the sword that was still lodged in his chest and pulled it outward, more blood surging from his lips and dripping onto the snow. He wriggled the blade free and took it skillfully by its hilt. The others, living and cursed, watched as he plunged it through the gap in the soldier's helmet, the blade sinking between his opened eyes and into the root behind his head. Solemn Woods was soon filled with the sounds of slaughter. Fresh human blood once more marked the black bark, and the agonized cries of grown men aware of their immediate doom pierced the winter twilight.

The observatory was just ahead. Rowan limped on his wounded leg and managed to catch his breath as he clutched the gate. He bowed his head and closed his eyes, listening numbly to the wicked grunts and cackles of the grotesque army that moved toward the edges of the woods behind him. The grounds were vacant.

"And how is it," a soldier with a dented helmet barked, as he clamored up to join him, "that you didn't foresee that?"

He was equally disheveled, his armor damaged and his temple crusted with blood. His sword, however, was colored with a darker, blacker blood than his own.

"It's safe here," Rowan told him, limping through the gate.

"Safer than the hollowed trunk you hid in while the others were murdered, seer?" the soldier snarled.

They climbed the steps. The great ancient door at the observatory's entrance was pulverized. The iron straps were singed and curled at the ends, and a giant, ragged opening revealed the dark hall inside.

"What magic did this?" Rowan whispered to himself.

"On with it," said the soldier, jutting his sword forward. "Of course, you know I expect double my fee given the circumstances. You led us to a ground no human should tread and I'll take my compensation."

"This is a cause greater than compensation," Rowan said. "My Order won't listen to me. I have foreseen ill will here for weeks. This will affect all of Salyndria, and something must be done." Rowan closed his hand into a fist. He made no reply and went inside. The soldier followed. Rowan called his light spell and tracked through the deserted common room. His impulse led him to the staircase. He paused to place his hand on the stone of its archway. Kyler's face flickered before him, enraged and frantic. She was racing up steps two by two and glancing over her shoulder.

"This way," he said, and they continued to climb.

The observatory was like a crypt—quiet, cold, and stagnant. Until they reached the third floor, there were no signs of life. Firelight glimmered in an open doorway. The smell was a mix of burnt wood and blood. The study they entered was demolished. The stone walls were pock-marked with large, charred craters and much of the furniture was either toppled over or broken. Glass bottles lay in shards on the ground. Rowan finally spotted the open marble box and the heap of scrolls. He rushed toward it while the soldier prodded disdainfully at his findings with the end of his sword.

"He's done it," Rowan gasped to himself, as he ran his fingers over the edges of the box. "He's really done it."

It was then that he sensed the body behind him. Turning, he saw Leith's wasted figure on the floor, black robes burnt at the chest and crusted blood in his ears and hair. Rowan dropped to him.

"Lord Leith?" he exclaimed, examining him with alarm.

The sorcerer was unmoving and pale, not the picture of sinister power Rowan had imagined. He envisioned a tall, dark, fiendish man with enchanted eyes, glittering velvet and an invincible affect. The man before him could have been mistaken for a homeless vagrant. The soldier's attention was roused, and he clattered over to get a better look. Rowan was checking Leith for signs of life, touching his forehead and finding it cold. He placed a hand on the sorcerer's chest, waited for it to expand with breath. There was nothing. Rowan's brow wrinkled as he looked at him. *The spell*, he thought.

"It's the same spell," he whispered, staring at the burnt robes.

"What are you blathering about?" barked the soldier.

"The incineration spell. That's what happened to the walls," Rowan explained, waving a hand at the deep craters in the stone. Rowan turned back to Leith and ripped open his robes. On the sorcerer's chest were no wounds or bruises—just old scars smeared with soot from the charred velvet. "It's impossible. He must have placed a protection charm on himself, and a powerful one. He should have been scorched right through!" Rowan declared in awe.

The scarred chest suddenly heaved. Rowan shouted in alarm and sprang backwards. The sorcerer's eyes were still closed, but breath came and left him steadily. Before their eyes, Leith's color returned and his ringed fingers twitched.

"He's alive!" Rowan exclaimed.

The soldier grinned, then raised his sword. "Not for long," he declared from within the helmet.

"Wait," Rowan ordered. *"Wait!"*

The soldier ignored him and advanced on Leith. He stood over him with a blood-tipped blade at his throat. Rowan pleaded for his retreat and tried to pull at the soldier's armored wrist to stop him.

Leith's stark eyes suddenly opened. "Invertium!" he whispered weakly at the sight of the sword at his neck.

Before Rowan's eyes, the sword reversed its structure: the blade became the hilt, and the hilt became the blade. The soldier yelped as he dropped it with a loud clang and nursed his bloodied hand. In an instant, Leith had launched to his feet. The soldier was sobered, angry, and ready to fight. He attacked, taking two quick, powerful swings at Leith, who dodged the first and blocked the second, then gripped the soldier's arm and twisted it around his back. In a blink, Leith's other arm had snaked around the soldier's neck and snapped it. In only a matter of seconds, the soldier had joined his fallen brethren in death.

The man fell to the floor in a clamor of noisy metal, his head turned unnaturally far to the side. Rowan froze in horror. Leith looked up at him. Before he could flee, Leith had pinned him to the wall, enraged hands squeezing at his throat.

"Who are you?" Leith demanded. "Who sent you?"

"Please!" Rowan choked out. "Kyler!"

Leith's face changed. His eyes opened wide, his lips parting as his fingers relented. "Kyler," he repeated in a coarse whisper. "Where is she?" he added, his rage returning.

"I don't know!" Rowan wheezed. "I'm from the Chamber of Sight. I thought she might be in danger so I came to take her away," he admitted weakly.

Leith looked at the boy, then released him. "You must be Rowan," he said, then glanced out the window toward the sound of a distant, howling scream. Rowan rubbed his neck and took a few deep breaths. Leith examined the room, eyeing the holes in the wall and the ravaged furniture. "Well, Rowan," said the sorcerer bitterly. "You've chosen a fine time to involve yourself. My treacherous assistant and her undead legion advance on your chamber as we speak."

"I knew it!" Rowan blurted, with an accusing point of his finger.

Leith seized him by the collar and dragged him, still struggling for breath, to the table. He picked up a cup near some scrolls. "Kyler drank from this before the ritual," he said, thrusting it at him. With that, he jerked on the collar so Rowan was face to face with his commanding blue eyes. "Find her."

There was a brass-colored glow over the landscape. Wickham stood at his balcony, his eyes on the snow-dusted hills that rolled down to the ink spot that was Solemn Woods. A wind came up to meet him, stirring the white wisps of his long beard and fluttering his decorated scarlet robe. There was a knock at the door.

"Enter!" the old man shouted over his shoulder.

A middle-aged female attendant came out to the balcony and stood at his side after a short bow. "You requested me, my lord," she said.

"Yes. Order the soldiers to their posts. Tell them to fully arm the battlements," Wickham told her, his eyes still on the hillside.

"Headmaster?" the woman almost laughed. "You jest, surely," she said.

"I do not," Wickham stated. "Do as I tell you. The darkest evil approaches. See how the twilight loiters," he said, waving a hand at the saffron light. "Rally our most decorated students. We will need our wits about us this night. Give the order," said Wickham, finally looking at her. The woman's face was blank with fear and shock. *"Now,"* the headmaster told her.

With a bewildered bow, she vanished, the heavy door booming closed behind her as a chorus of panicked voices was muffled in the hallway. Wickham looked back out at the land. The woods stirred, its outskirts flickering with movement. They would make their way up the hills soon. They would have their revenge.

"Come now, my old friend," the old man said to the air. "You must not disappoint me."

Rowan and Leith stood in the shadowed dome, the Lunathyl symbols on the conduit glowing faintly. The bats were unusually quiet. Rowan held the cup in both hands. Leith held the collar of the boy's robe in his fist.

"You're sure," Leith said.

"She came up here," Rowan confirmed. "She was afraid. She used that," he said, nodding at the conduit. "Where does it lead?"

"An underground passage to Lamentiose," Leith explained.

"Lamentiose! So, it's true! You've ruined us all, do you hear?" Rowan cried. "Only the gods know what the Hypnogoths have done to her!" he said.

"Nothing worse than I'll do to you if your mewling doesn't cease!" Leith snarled, yanking on the boy's robe.

Rowan hushed, Leith's eyes flashing at him. Leith stepped up onto the conduit.

"Oh, no. Not me," Rowan said, pulling back. "We haven't power over them, don't you understand? They will make madmen out of us, trap us in nightmares."

Leith's lip curled with annoyance, and he tugged hard on the boy's robe, pulling him up onto the slab with him. The echoes of Rowan's protests lingered as they both dissipated in a puff of shining powder.

Torch flames lit the dirt corridor where they reappeared. Rowan fell to the ground, face first, where he coughed and rolled, while trying to nurse his head and chest. Leith was calm and alert, standing still on the circle of runes and eyeing the long tunnel carefully. It was empty. Leith hoisted the boy to his feet and started down the passage.

"Keep on your toes, seer," Leith warned over his shoulder.

"You're not listening," Rowan persisted, skipping to keep up. "They'll kill us."

"Unless this is one of your vivid predictions," Leith said, "kindly be silent."

"What do you plan to do?" Rowan asked after a moment.

"They will want their gauntlet back," said Leith. "They know I am the only one capable enough to retrieve it. Hypnogoths are shrewd negotiators."

"Negotiators?" Rowan echoed, a high pitch in his voice.

"Has the focus on history at the Academy grown so lax since my exile?" Leith said. "Ages ago, the Hypnogoths were Salyndria's foulest nuisance. They roamed the countryside looting treasure and anyone who tried to stop them fell victim to their power. Their guardianship over Lamentiose was the kingdom's most brilliant appointment: a massive hoard of enchanted relics and weapons arrive with every fallen sorcerer-criminal's coffin, and the Hypnogoths are allowed to protect it with as much vehemence as they wish."

"You're going to speak with them," Rowan said skeptically.

"No doubt they are keeping Kyler for an exchange. They'll have terms. I must try to persuade them to let me take her back. Unless you foresee my failure," Leith added with a tinge of mocking.

"I want to save her, too," Rowan defended. "Kyler and I are very close." Leith ignored his declaration, walking ahead. "I love her," he finally blurted, stopping in his tracks.

Leith halted, as well. He turned and faced the boy. "Do you?" He asked dryly, his eyes gleaming blue in the tunnel's shadows.

"Yes," he answered shakily.

"Then you would have kept her away from Solemn Woods," Leith told him, before resuming his trek down the root-crossed passage.

Rowan was still, staring after the blot of black velvet that moved like a giant bat wing along the intermittent torch flames. He looked down into the cup, tracing the brim with his finger before he raced after Leith.

At last, they reached the round chamber where Leith had made his crude entryway into the ceiling. Still, there were no signs of life. Quietly, Leith motioned for Rowan to climb the platform, to which he shook his head 'no', then reluctantly complied when Leith took only one determined step toward him. Soon they both stood in the antechamber, bathed in silvery torch light and surrounded by the white walls. The door that led outside to the island was wide open.

"May the gods save us!" Rowan whispered in awe.

The mist undulated outside the door, clearing as they approached to reveal a set of stone steps that led down the steep hill on which the mausoleum sat. From the doorway, the view of Lamentiose was grand before them, its vast, lead-colored hills steeped in fog with huge, dead trees and the tops of gravestones peeking out. The twilight was garish on the ground.

"Come on," Leith said, as he made his way down the steps.

Rowan's eyes darted left and right at the mist, and with a reluctant whimper, he followed. Their figures seemed to swim in the fog, and when they reached the bottom of the hill, the glimmering light from the mausoleum doorway was still visible above. Leith stood a moment, studying the surroundings. There were two trees, their trunks dried and ashen, along with small patches of withered weeds and a crumbling stone bench among several headstones. Leith called his light spell.

The fog retreated from around them and Rowan took a step back. Leith waited.

"What do you sense?" he asked Rowan, who had faithfully held on to Kyler's cup.

"She's here, but . . ." Rowan held the vessel in both hands, his thin brows knitted with confusion: "*Not* here. I sense her, but it's faint. She's unharmed," he added with surprise. "It's strange. I can't explain it," said Rowan, shaking his head at the misted knolls.

"Shh!" Leith halted him, raising a hand.

Something moved in the fog. It was a dark figure among the headstones. Both men were rigid and silent as it approached. It was tall and erect, unlike the Hypnogoths' hunched, contorted frames. As it neared Leith's light, a hooded face appeared, pale and beautiful in the moon-like glow. Long brown tresses spilled out from the edges of the hood and a round medallion caught the twilight.

"Kyler!" Rowan exclaimed. He dropped the cup and moved toward her.

Leith held out an arm to stop him. "Wait!" he ordered fiercely.

They stared at the woman before them, familiar, but not. She smiled softly, almost wickedly. The eyes were no longer hazel, but a luminous yellow. Her arms were at her sides, the hands curled slightly into stiff claws. She spoke:

"You have something that belongs to us." Kyler's smooth, feminine tone was overlapped by a grotesque, growl-like pitch. "I hope you've come to make a bargain."

Rowan's eyes opened wide in horror. Leith lowered his arm and stepped forward.

"The girl is innocent," he said. "Whatever crime you want to punish her for is my doing. I've corrupted her judgment."

The creature chuckled, sneering widely with Kyler's willowy lips. "She is with us," it said. "And her judgment is her own. She is like us." It paused to raise a twisted hand at Leith, indicating his inclusion. "A child of nightshade. We are prone to dark desires. Nythos, however, is displeased."

"Let her go," Leith demanded.

"Make a bargain," the Hypnogoth repeated, the claw-like hand retreating to rest on Kyler's amulet. "You've taken our gauntlet. Bring it home to us, or we will keep something of yours to replace it. Don't pretend that she means nothing to you, sorcerer," it said, taking down the hood of Kyler's cloak.

At this, Rowan turned to Leith, who looked away from the Hypnogoth's yellow eyes.

"Let her go and I will bring back what I've stolen," he answered.

The Hypnogoth laughed, Kyler's pretty head falling back with its shrill cackling. Suddenly, the laughter of the others, watching from somewhere among the crypts and cemetery trees shrouded in mist, rang out around him.

"We are amused," it said. "Your task is a difficult one. Should our treasure fall into your hands once more, are your affections strong enough to guide you back to Lamentiose to save her? Or will you decide the gauntlet is what you cannot part with?"

Leith did not respond. Rowan looked on without speaking.

"Your time wanes," the Hypnogoth said after a moment, then turned to head into the mist.

"Wait," Leith called after it. The creature ignored him. "Wait!" he said again. Once more, the two men were alone in the graveyard.

Leith extinguished his light as the fog crept back over the ground and engulfed them. "Let's go," Leith said finally, turning toward the steps. "And hurry."

CHAPTER TEN

THE SIEGE

The Chamber of Sight cast a long shadow on the sloping hill. In its rising shade an army moved, a worming mass of living dead advancing. Clad only in tattered robes, their faces wounded, filthy, and scabbed, they came with frosted eyes and grinning mouths. They had assembled at the forest entrance and were now shifting forward up the hill. The high chamber walls came alive with torches, armed soldiers at the ready and a line of archers holding fast. Students watched in horror from the bastions, clutching each other in fear as the sun finally inched toward the horizon.

Wickham stood behind a row of archers. They waited for the first of the cursed legion to come into range. Down in the growing darkness of the hill there was a tiny beacon, blue sparks of lightning at a point that followed behind the army. High-pitched cackling echoed.

"What is that?" a commander asked, stepping forward toward the edge of the wall. Suddenly there was the sound of a hundred howls and chants that filled the night like ominous thunder. The archers shifted nervously.

"Steady!" the commander urged.

The figures were visible now, their pale, wasted forms like something from a nightmare, rigid and fearless with military poise despite ragged, disheveled frocks and weaponless hands. Their vicious laughter pierced the evening. In the torchlight several of them spit on the ground and gestured up at the soldiers. Others tore off their robes, revealing sickly, ashen skin marked with scars. The soldiers were breathing heavier now, the steam rapidly escaping from their mouths into the cold air.

"They will climb," Wickham advised the commander. "Make it difficult for them."

The commander nodded. "Ready!" he said to the archers. "Aim for the limbs!" Thirty arrows aligned in the firelight.

A wave of grunting and hissing rang out, and the cursed army lurched forward toward the walls.

"Fire!"

There was a mighty snap and the moonlight shined briefly on the sharpened arrowheads as they left their bows and sailed into the night. They rained down on the grotesque figures, many of whom had already started clawing at the high stone wall. The muted thump of impact filled the air as the arrows pierced flesh and bone. No cries of pain followed, only aggravated snarling. Several who had made progress three feet up fell from the force, while others tried to get a footing, their efforts impeded by the arrows sticking out of their thighs.

Wickham leaned over the wall. A few were staring up at him with their milky, expressionless eyes. Those who had been struck paused, then systematically began breaking off the ends of the arrows in their arms, legs, and feet. There were two who were still on the wall, slowly and awkwardly climbing up. One of them had an arrow straight through his head. What troubled him most was that not all of them had charged the chamber's wall—a line of about twenty held back, waiting. Wickham's thick white brows furrowed. The little blue spark of light was still visible behind the army.

"We need magic," he said gravely.

Suddenly, a spell rang out—voices gritty and sinister chanted the same word in unison, like a chorus. It came from the line that remained, its vengeful growl hitting the air like a heavy drumbeat.

"Ascendo!" they said.

Wickham and the soldiers stared in horror as the animated corpses lifted from the ground and came soaring up toward them.

Leith led the way out of Solemn Woods. He would not use his orb, so he and Rowan made their way through the black trees by streaks of moonlight. Beyond the forest's edge, the hill was vacant and grim. They treaded forward past the thin patches of dry grass and birches until they came to a halt at the top of the hill. The chamber was before them, figures thrashing on the battlements and climbing the walls like spiders. Screaming and cries of anguish echoed.

Somewhere in the midst of it all, Leith heard laughter.

He shot quickly down the hill toward the cover of a small thicket. Rowan followed, bewildered. Leith hit the ground flat on his stomach, his eyes on the gauntlet's glowing spark, visible through a panel of dead branches. Rowan copied him.

"The chamber!" Rowan cried frantically. "It's under attack!"

"Shhh!" Leith ordered, then pointed at the light.

"What's that?" Rowan asked.

"Marisele. She has the gauntlet," Leith answered in a whisper. "And it looks like your chamber will belong to her soon if we don't stop her."

"How do we do that?" Rowan said with dismay.

Leith paused, his eyes busy with thought as he surveyed their surroundings through the frame of bushes.

"When I tell you, you'll wish I'd killed you back at the observatory," he answered, then rose to his knees, where he shuffled in his robes for several magical items.

"What?" Rowan blurted loudly.

"Unless you want to die before that," Leith hissed angrily, gripping his protest in his throat, "for the last time, bite your tongue. If she hears us, the stocks will seem like paradise compared to the punishment she'll levy."

With that, Leith let go and continued gathering his items. Rowan took a few wheezing breaths and bitterly collected himself.

"What have you planned?" he asked, rubbing his neck.

"You'll distract her while I try out some spells," said Leith.

"*Try out?* Are you a madman? No, I don't even have to ask that," Rowan said.

"That gauntlet is too powerful. I don't know what opposition I pose, if any. All I can do is use my most effective incantations against her and hope they work," Leith explained, holding a small pouch to his ear and shaking it.

"And what am I to do? Juggle apples for her?" Rowan asked cynically.

Leith paused, then looked at him squarely. His eyes were brightly lit cobalt in the shadow of the thicket.

"You tried to have me killed," he reminded. "By all rights, you should be lying next to your behemoth friend in my study. Your usefulness to me is the only reason you're not. Think of something," Leith said, then left the thicket.

The Chamber of Sight was overrun. The archers, out of arrows, fled to the towers. The soldiers had killed only a few of their foes by decapitation before being smothered by more. The bastion walkways were littered with bodies—some the headless corpses of the enemy, arrows stuck everywhere; others the mangled forms of the soldiers and students who had tried magic. Only a handful of soldiers remained, two of them escorting Headmaster Wickham, whom they had rushed from danger at the onset of the attack, to his quarters.

The sounds of fighting and death were on all sides of him as they raced through the passages. Several times his escorts stopped to fight off an ambush of ash-skinned fiends who had been roaming the halls in search of more victims. With the quick slice of a blade they lay headless on the floor, their white eyes dim and expired.

"You must go," Wickham had been repeating to them. "Save yourselves. They will be searching for me," he tried to explain, but the soldiers ignored him, pulling him gingerly along until they were outside his heavy oak door.

"Stay here, Headmaster," one advised, before closing him inside.

Wickham was alone in his chamber, a winter wind rushing up from the balcony. The echoes of fighting and dying came with it. The brave men who guarded his door would not be alive much longer.

In the moonlight, Leith was a black specter moving stealthily along the flank of birches toward the gauntlet's beacon. Rowan cursed quietly as he followed. They moved up behind Marisele, between the thin birches under the cover of night. She stood on a small rock formation, the light from the gauntlet bright as day about her. Leith nodded at Rowan, who reluctantly stepped out into the clearing where the witch was guiding her army. The chaos of the siege could be heard not far away—the shout of commands, the whir of flying arrows, and the clink of steel. Rowan cautiously approached, his shoulders hunched. He cleared his throat.

"I ask your pardon, Madam!" he said to her. The forks of electricity that engulfed the gauntlet crackled. "A moment, if you please?"

Marisele jerked back the hood of her worn antique robe. Her gossamer hair spilled out. The arm that wore the gauntlet was streaked with trails of dried blood that stained her sleeve.

"How foolishly bold is Wickham's brood!" she shrieked with laughter. "Don't you know how quick your death can be delivered?"

"I represent the Chamber of Sight," Rowan began diplomatically. "I've come on behalf of the Academy to ask that you cease this incursion. We ask for your prudence in the matter as your cooperation will guarantee that . . . oh!"

His speech was interrupted as he was swiftly levitated several feet in the air. Marisele controlled him with her hand, turning him upside down over a rock.

"What spell have you now, boy? Let's see it," she said.

"Please!" Rowan begged, looking below him at the jagged boulder that would crack his skull should she release him.

"Give your god, Videus, my regards!" Marisele said, then pulled back her arm.

Rowan's outcry filled the night as he dropped headfirst toward the rock.

"Modifus!" Leith's grating shout echoed from somewhere behind the trees and the rock became a tall pile of leaves onto which Rowan fell. Marisele's watchful eye flicked toward the trees. Before she could raise her gauntlet, his voice rang out again. "Fulminato!" he said, and a great round fireball soared toward the witch, blasting her in the chest and knocking her from the rock.

Rowan crawled from the leaves and raced toward the trees. Marisele shook her head and stood slowly. As she did, she cackled loudly, burning embers visible on her robe, the gauntlet still bright with its charge.

"So you survived!" she said to the darkness. "Do you truly think you can thwart me now? Malantheus's power courses through me. Do your worst, reject!" A fierce blast of blue lightning streaked toward the trees.

Leith moved quickly out of view, the explosion leaving a massive, charred void in the cluster of white birches. Rowan dropped to the ground, crawling carefully around the witch. She lit up the night with two more probing blasts, one that sailed right over Rowan's head to impact the trees just a few feet away. Leith whirled around the tree and scaled the hill toward her with what looked like a fistful of something. At the edge of the birches he crouched, then hurled powder into the air.

Instantly, a chorus of chirping overlapped the sounds of battle further up the hill. The powder morphed into a huge cloud of a hundred angry bats that swarmed Marisele. The light from the gauntlet dimmed behind the mass of black wings, and the old witch screamed and flailed in panic. As she ran toward the chamber, Rowan took the moment to race over to where Leith stood. Both men waited to see if his spell had been successful. The hag had stopped and was crying out in agony, the bats likely nipping at her exposed flesh.

Suddenly, her crackling voice rang out again. "Comburo!"

A ball of green light appeared, then expanded outward from Marisele into a spherical shield that immediately burned up each bat it touched, their black bodies making tiny sparks as they were turned to ash like popping embers in the night.

"Damn," Leith said.

"Congregum Decum Summonus!" her voice pealed, as she raised an arm at the chamber walls.

"What's she doing now?" Rowan asked.

"Calling ten of her army back from battle," Leith answered grimly. "This will be harder than I thought."

Wickham looked down from the balcony. Below him on the bastion walls, the soldiers stabbed at their enemies only to draw their swords back dry. They were overcome, some fleeing and some slicing away as the dead tore them apart. Several of the soldiers had learned to lop off arms and legs to finally halt them, which resulted in a grotesque scene of blood-soaked walkways littered with severed limbs and half-bodies still jerking and crawling with determination.

The battle had extended onto the field. The gate was raised, and more soldiers poured out to finish those who'd fallen from the wall and gain a vantage point to aim arrows at the overrun bastions. Wickham glanced back at his heavy door, gazing at the worn carving and listening for the voices of the guards who stood outside.

More cries of death called his attention back to the view. Two of Marisele's soldiers—a purple-robed girl and white-robed man—had just killed an officer with his own sword down on the hill. Both had numerous arrows jutting out of their shoulders and backs.

Then something stopped them, evidently calling their interest. Slowly, they turned from the dead officer and headed calmly down the hill, the girl still clutching the sword in her hand. They were on their way to the blue beacon, which had drawn closer now. Wickham gripped the railing as he listened to the muffled sounds of combat outside his door. He withdrew into his chambers, keeping his eyes on the door as it quaked on its ancient hinges. The sounds were unmistakable. There was a long outcry of defeat, then two thumps. His guards were dead.

Marisele stood on the hill as the last of the ten she'd summoned marched up behind her to join the line. Leith and Rowan remained at the edge of the trees. She and her army were unmoving. It was a challenge.

"This looks bad," Rowan remarked.

"I have to get that gauntlet," Leith reminded.

"What other spells do you know?" Rowan asked.

"None that she can't send back at me tenfold."

"What are we going to do?"

Leith didn't answer. He stared out from the trees at her ten accomplices and rubbed his chin. After a moment, he spoke. "There is one spell that would finish her for good, but I have to get closer to her. I have to be able to touch her," he explained.

"Oh, well there you have it, everything's sorted," Rowan snorted sarcastically. "How do you propose . . .?"

"Your outlook is beginning to irritate me," Leith said through clenched teeth. "I fear I don't have a choice. I must simply go to meet her."

"She'll kill you!" Rowan said.

On the end of Rowan's words, Leith was already on his way up the hill. He maneuvered between several large boulders, which he planned to use as cover if things didn't go his way. So far, Marisele made no move. She chuckled lightly as Leith approached. Her army stared, white-eyed, sneering, and covered in blood. One of them was missing an arm.

"I should have assumed you'd fortified your robes," she said. "I won't make that mistake again."

"You've won," Leith told her. "You've outwitted me—and I applaud you."

Marisele's eye squinted in suspicion. "What is this trickery now? You think your words will bring you mercy? Never have I seen you submit, my lord, to anyone but Nythos."

"In light of this battle you will have control of the Orders," Leith said. "You know how vehemently I've pursued this cause. You know I have no loyalty to the Academy. If I cannot have the power for myself, I will serve the one who has secured it." With this, Leith dropped to one knee. "You were my ward, now I shall be yours."

A hiss came from Marisele's throat. She was perplexed. "Lying fiend! Surely you can't mean this."

"After all we have been through together, how can I not now recognize my purpose? What choice have I? You've left me with nothing. At least grant me the chance to serve you well," said Leith.

He bowed silently for a moment. Marisele remained still, the gauntlet sparking with its charge.

Then she cackled loudly, tossing her head back. He had not convinced her. Leith saw his chance and reached out, attempting to touch her feet as a token of his submission. His fingers reached her weathered boots. "Identium Ostendo!" Leith said.

Instantly, Marisele winced back to focus, looked down at Leith, and kicked his hand away. But it was too late. Already, her hair was turning from white to black, the fraying wisps smoothing out around her shoulders. She stumbled briefly.

In the moon's glow, Marisele's old robes were renewed, the ruby fabric now shining and the tears closing up. Her flesh was rejuvenated, the wrinkles vanished, and the color returned to her cheeks. The age melted from her, revealing a tall, handsome young woman with dramatic angular features and long, flowing hair the color of oil. The eye was still absent, but the wound was fresh, crisscrossed by wine-colored scabs under her set of skewed black brows. She heaved urgent breaths as she slowly realized what was happening to her. Marisele glanced down at her hands as the skin turned from dry and shriveled to polished and smooth.

"What . . . what is this?" she whispered, suddenly marveling at her own transformation. Her now supple lips formed a smile and she touched her face and hair with delight. "By the gods!" she squealed, hearing her own voice without its cracking and scraping. Her bliss left her quickly, and she glared at Leith with suspicion. "What have you done?"

Instantly, Leith was tossed back by a violent shock as she brought the gauntlet down to strike him in the shoulder. He growled loudly from the pain. Hurriedly, he rolled to the left to dodge one of her lightning streaks that melted the snow and blackened the ground.

Leith got to his feet and retreated toward the rocks, hearing more attacks behind him and feeling the ground pulse with them. Into the thickening darkness he ran, guided only by the blue outlines of the rocks on his left and right. Suddenly, he tripped and fell forward, nearly hit by a streak that sailed over his head and struck a rock in front of him. Leith's enchanted vision revealed Rowan crouched behind a boulder next to him. It was the seer who'd tripped him. Leith scrambled to join him behind the rock and groped through his robes for more magical items.

"I fear we need a new strategy," Leith grumbled, angrily tossing empty pouches into the snow. "I've got nothing left but petty charms."

"There's no time, we have to go," Rowan said, breathless and frantic. "Come on! Go, go, go!" he said, then leapt from behind the boulder toward the trees.

Leith obeyed, following the boy's cobalt silhouette. Behind him, there was a great rushing sound like an avalanche. The two of them ducked into the trees and turned to watch a massive wave of gray smoke billow up and over the rocks where they had been hiding. There was a hissing sound, the snow vanishing and the rocks giving off trails of white fumes.

"Acid gas," Rowan breathed, holding onto a tree. "I foresaw it."

"What about this?" Leith said, pointing at Marisele's line of cohorts who were raising their arms in unison with her.

Points of light appeared at their hands and shot toward Leith and Rowan like arrows. Eleven tiny glowing orbs came toward them. Leith and Rowan parted and dropped to the ground, the balls striking the trees and snow like meteors. Both men dodged each subsequent attack, Leith maneuvering skillfully between the thin birches until he heard Rowan wail in pain. The attacks ceased as Marisele and her army of ten advanced on them. Leith rushed over to where Rowan lay at the edge of the woods.

Rowan's thin brows were bent with suffering. One of the orbs had struck him in the shoulder, where he clasped his hand over the bleeding wound. Leith kneeled down and propped him up against a tree.

"Don't move, I'll lead her away," Leith said sternly.

"No!" Rowan struggled to protest. He winced and squeezed his shoulder, then collected himself again. "Don't lead her away. Keep her close. She's right where she needs to be. We just need a little more time."

"What are you talking about?" Leith snarled impatiently.

Just then, Marisele's gauntlet lit up the birches, their thin, white trunks like bony fingers in the azure glow. Leith turned.

"How tragic," the witch said, her now lovely features bright with triumph, "that this is how you'll be remembered in the history books—the fool who fell for trickery and tried to resist Malantheus' army, murdered with ease after all his greatest spells failed him." Leith tensed. His heart thundered and he closed his injured hand into a fist. "You'll have much to tell the gods, Master Leith," Marisele said, as she raised the gauntlet, aiming it at him.

More time. Leith stood slowly, his head bowed. "At least I will die having finally seen your beauty," he said.

Something stopped her. The woman looked suddenly confused. She laughed again. "What did you say?"

"If I have treated you terribly, it was only to fight my own feelings." Leith dropped to his knees again. "Imagine my shame in loving a gnarled old woman. Kyler was a welcome distraction. I ask your forgiveness now, please, before you send me to oblivion."

Marisele scoffed, but as he looked up at her, he saw a glint of weakness. "Deceptive to the last," she said, but without much conviction.

"I could have been rid of you long ago if it weren't true," Leith said. "I know you feel the same. I only wish I could . . ."

"What?" Marisele pressed angrily.

It was in this moment that Leith gathered up his wits to gaze at her, taking in her young, beautiful figure in the moonlight. He surveyed her, imagining that she was Kyler before him, wanting to hold her in his arms once more.

"I only wish I could have had you like this," he said, his eyes on her body. "Just once."

The witch stared at him. He kept his eyes on her body, deliberately eyeing the curves of her hips, the folds of her robes over her breasts. His eyes finally met hers as his gaze traveled upward. Her lips were curved in a conflicted frown. He could see her chest heaving as her breathing quickened. The sparks from the gauntlet suddenly dimmed.

"I . . ." she stammered.

His seduction was having its effect on her magic. Just then, her face changed. She winced as if struck by sudden pain. The gauntlet jerked on her arm, sparking with its dimmed lightning and acting as if of its own accord to free itself of her. Marisele cried out with discomfort, the spikes likely tearing at her flesh from its underside. The stolen sword that was held by the girl in the purple robe suddenly leapt from her hand and sailed past Leith and Rowan into the trees. Leith felt his own hand being pulled by some force. He gripped it tightly by his wrist, watching his rings slide from his fingers and fly after the sword.

"No!" cried Marisele, as she tried to anchor the gauntlet with her other hand. But it pulled at her skin and yanked her forward. She wrapped one arm around a nearby tree to halt herself, her gauntlet arm pulling back in midair as if she were about to cast another spell. "Help me!" she turned to say to her minion, who only stared back blankly. She howled in agony as the steel glove tore at her, desperate to detach.

"Take it off!" Leith ordered.

"No! Desisto!" Marisele shouted, but to no effect. The spikes had left her, their deep red scratches leaving a trail down her arm as the glove slid further off. "Desisto!"

The gauntlet was ripped from her, and she screamed as if she were being skinned alive, the flesh of her arm lacerated and dripping with blood. The relic soared into the darkness, leaving the traces of its beam between the trees.

CHAPTER ELEVEN

BLACK ROBES

Headmaster Wickham winced as the great wooden door shuddered on its iron hinges. It rattled with every blow, debris flaking from the walls and frame as it was struck violently from outside. The old man stepped backward behind a chair, gripping it as if it was his defender. The door bulged inward, the straps warping and bending until they dropped to the floor, along with their thick bolts. Finally, it broke open, hideous laughter pouring in as the dust settled. Several pairs of white eyes greeted him. The nightmarish undead members of the Black Trade grinned menacingly, their antique robes in thin scraps about them.

Two of them held a large statue horizontally, taken from the hallway and used as a battering ram. They dropped it and stepped into the headmaster's quarters. Wickham was still, his posture straight as they advanced toward him. But the grins abruptly left the cracked lips and wilted faces. Each of them halted in mid-step, their interests turning from the headmaster. It was as if they felt a bite or sting somewhere on their bodies. They winced and turned to each other, puzzled. In seconds they had begun to change: their eyes faded from opaque white to red pinpoints of irises, and their flesh took on a grayer, more translucent hue.

Whatever injuries they'd suffered vanished, their scrapes and stabs closing up, the haggard corpses returning to their cursed ghostly forms. Wickham stepped out from behind the chair. They looked up at him, desperate and despairing.

"You have no power here, now," he said to them calmly. The sounds of battle beyond his balcony had hushed. "Your era has ended. Return to your resting place. Your absolution waits for you."

The ghosts gawked at him, then looked at each other. The soldiers rejoiced outside, hollering with relief. They must have discovered their new advantage. Wickham glanced out the window. The dark army had dissolved into small clouds of black mist, which collected and hovered over the chamber like toxic fog. Then, like a whirlwind, it funneled toward the woods from atop the bastion walls. Wickham looked back at his chamber. His invaders had gone. Only a wisp of black mist remained on his threshold, which was quickly drawn out the window and sucked up by the night. He rushed to the balcony to watch it flee past the torchlight.

The slain bodies of the others morphed into fog, leaving only their blood and the corpses of the soldiers they'd killed on the stone next to them. Soon it had all vanished, the walls and walkways clear in the firelight. The soldiers, somewhat bewildered, tracked the bastions looking for any strays and tending to their fallen. Wickham turned to his desk, gathered up some items from the drawers, and rushed through his broken doorway.

Marisele was still howling, her bleeding hand still outstretched. Her army waited, the will of their cause absent from their faces. Suddenly, a few of them jerked forward. The arrows that were stuck in their torsos and arms burst out, leaving their bodies and flying into the woods as if they had been summoned. Mystified, they patted their wounds and looked around at the darkness.

"What's happening?" Rowan whispered.

Leith's luminous eyes narrowed. The army began to change before him. The wounds seemed to suck up all the blood, then closed in as if the arrows never touched them. His eyes revealed their dimming forms and the solid, walking corpses became filmy, ashen specters once again. The whites of their eyes darkened and their unnatural senses returned. The faces dull with Marisele's drone will gained back their tortured, otherworldly vigor. Leith held his breath. The sound of rushing wind pierced the night, and a wave of thick, dark fog soared over the hill, where it settled around the others.

The fog began to clear quickly as the rest of the army materialized from it. They appeared from behind and between the first ten, forming twenty, then thirty, then sixty. Soon, a hoard of them took up the hillside. Malantheus' followers had regained their curse. They were no longer walking flesh, but ghosts once more. Leith looked up at Marisele, who was still leaning against the tree, bemoaning her loss.

But the sound of her army halted her malaise. They were gathered at the edge of the woods, staring with astonished acknowledgment at the witch who had failed them. It was a few of them at first, one or two calling out her name. Then it grew louder, more furious, until it became a war cry that split the night. The spell that returned her to her youth had made her recognizable to the army she betrayed so long ago. The gauntlet no longer protected her, nor did it control them.

"Marisele of Umbra Vale! Marisele!" they chanted, her name like rolling thunder over the hillside.

The single eye opened wide with terror. She raised her hands to them. "No, no. You don't understand. My comrades!" she pleaded, stepping backwards.

Leith turned to Rowan, who still gripped his hurt shoulder.

"What's happening?" Rowan breathed.

"They know who she is. And they aren't pleased," he said. "Can you walk?"

"I think," Rowan said.

Leith quickly helped him to his feet and they both rushed into the woods to gain their distance. Rowan called his flame, the light playing off the trunks of the trees and revealing Marisele's red-robed figure as she backed away from her legion. The two men watched the army advance on her, chanting "traitor" and snarling with wrath as her futile pleas echoed. Soon there were screams as they surrounded her, shrill and agonized as she vanished within the mass of them. Rowan gulped and turned his head.

"Kyler!" Leith shouted suddenly.

A few feet away, Kyler was seated against the base of a birch, a bundle of brown robes with her arms clutching something to her chest. Rowan held his light up and they rushed over. Leith dropped to the ground beside her. Her head was bowed.

"Kyler," he said to her, lifting her chin.

Her green eyes peered up at him. There was a charge about her, a low hum that pulsed and radiated. She cradled the gauntlet, which still sparked blue from under her long sleeves. She was weak and breathing heavily, the lids of her eyes half-closed.

"I'm sorry," she said. "I had to make a bargain."

As he examined her, Leith noticed his rings partially imbedded in the smooth flesh of her neck and collar. Her medallion was gone. The sword had just missed her, leaving a small slice in her shoulder. It was now stuck in the trunk of the birch, its long, steel blade curved toward her and the hilt cleaving to her arm. There were several arrows that decorated the tree as well, but Kyler hadn't been able to avoid them all. One had struck the other shoulder just below the collar bone. Blood trickled down from where it pierced her.

"What are you saying?" Leith asked her frantically. "What bargain?"

"I didn't believe you would come back for me," Kyler said. "I offered my medallion for the chance to retrieve it myself." She took a labored breath. "They let me go. I went to the laboratory. I doubled the potion."

Leith exhaled with despair and took up her face in his hands. "Abscido," he said, and the hum ceased. Kyler's expression softened; the strength of the magnetization potion had likely caused her a great deal of discomfort. "You'll be all right," Leith told her firmly, though he could hear his own voice shaking with fear. He turned to Rowan. "We need a healing spell," he said.

"I don't know any," Rowan choked out.

"There must be one," Leith snapped harshly.

Rowan took a step back. "She needs someone from the Order of Light," he answered weakly.

"And here is my punishment," Leith growled. "This is how you scold me, Nythos!" he said, looking up at the stars through the silhouette of treetops.

"Leith," Kyler breathed, her eyes closing.

"No," Leith said fiercely, taking her up in his arms. "No, no, stay with me!" he ordered. "Kyler, you'll be all right. Open your eyes!" She was limp against him, her body warm and her arms slack. He cradled her head in his hand, looking down at her lovely face while his blood rushed with desperation. He called her name and shook her once. Her thin brows twitched in response. "She needs help!" Leith barked at Rowan. "There must be someone at your wretched chamber who knows a spell that stops bleeding!"

"The problem with the Order of Shadow," said a voice from

somewhere among the trees, "is that defense and destruction are your only specialties." Headmaster Wickham stepped into Rowan's light, the old man's white beard streaked with soot and his decorated red robes dusted with debris. "It might serve the Academy better if, in the future, we diversify our chambers."

"Headmaster!" Rowan said, as he bowed shortly.

Leith leaned Kyler gently against the tree. "Headmaster," he said. "Please."

"Bring your light closer, Rowan," said Wickham, and the boy obeyed. Wickham kneeled, examining her. She stirred. "It's all right, child," he said, then curved his hand in a C-shape around the arrow wound. "Extricato," the old man said.

Leith was unsettled as Kyler let out a cry of pain and the arrow slowly inched its way out of her shoulder into Wickham's grasp. The headmaster tossed it aside and pulled back her robe to reveal the ugly puncture that now bled even more profusely. Placing his hand over it, he said, "Sangui Insulus."

Instantly, the flow stopped and the wound closed up into a scab encircled by a large bruise. Wickham reached into his robes and brought out clean rags. He began to clean off the wound. Kyler was pale and whimpering. The old man whispered soothing reassurances as he began to gingerly pluck the rings from her neck.

"Leith," he said. "Give me the gauntlet."

Leith blinked. "Headmaster?"

Wickham chuckled lightly as he continued his task. "How I enjoy the fruit of my predictions," he said. "I knew you would be fond of her, so fond that when the treasure you've spent years trying to claim is at your feet, that menacing mind of yours can only labor over her welfare."

Leith's eyes shifted. Realization found him and he turned on his knees. The gauntlet had rolled out of her grasp after he'd freed her from the effects of the magnetic potion. Even when he brought her into his embrace, he'd overlooked that it was now in his possession. The relic glowed on the ground, the sparks intermittent against the shadows of the thin birches. Leith gazed at it, scanning the years of his isolation in his mind like pages in a book. He shook his head.

"You knew," Leith's graveled voice echoed. "You knew everything, didn't you? This was no mistake, no plot to misguide me. The inscription in the tomb . . . ?"

"Centuries in the making, my deviant friend," Wickham told him.

"This is a prophecy," Rowan blurted.

"No," Wickham corrected. "This was an arrangement, a pact between the Academy and the priests of Amaleus. It was to be a matter of utmost secrecy. Fate would bring the pieces into play when the time was right." Wickham stopped to look up at Leith. "When your ambitions as a student became apparent, I knew then that the time was near. You don't think I exiled you to the observatory for its scenic location, do you?"

"There was no student with a vision," Rowan said somberly. "It was your own, wasn't it, Headmaster?"

"I'll take that gauntlet now," Wickham said.

Leith paused, looking at him suspiciously. "It has to be returned," he said firmly. "Kyler may have made her bargain, but the Hypnogoths still hold me to mine."

"Yes," Wickham agreed, pulling Kyler's robes back over her wound. "It is clear they have their grip on her still," he said, brushing her hair back from her face. Her brow was knitted as if from some nightmare, her eyes closed and her head rolling from side to side. "But you must call on trust once more, Leith, as you once did when you served us. Give me the gauntlet," Wickham repeated strictly, holding out his pale, wrinkled hand.

Leith surveyed him. The two men locked eyes, engaged in a dangerous exchange of unknown motives. He searched the headmaster's features, once sharply angled, now sagging slightly with age. Lush, level white brows partially obscured the knowing gaze. Wickham had been the only one to recognize the value of Leith's enterprises despite his crimes, the only headmaster who had always acted honorably, the only one who had shown him pardon. What did he want with the gauntlet? Was he simply waiting for the right moment, as Marisele had?

Leith's jaw clenched, and he reached behind him where the ground glowed. Something called him—Kyler's words—*Surely even you must sometimes miss the light.* That world flashed before him, the valor and brotherhood he once lived for pulsing in his blood. The thrill of assignment and his devotion to the kingdom had consumed him, then. But now, after all this time, could he once again find that will within him? Leith gripped the gauntlet and held it in front of him. He studied the markings in the metal and marveled at its ancient craftsmanship. It was his, finally, this gateway to the power he craved!

The piercing blue eyes flicked up at his superior. In a slow, languid movement, Leith placed it in Wickham's hand. The old man breathed out with relief and cautiously stood up. He turned his back on the three of them and headed toward the edge of the woods.

"Headmaster?" Rowan called. He continued without an answer, trudging on the light layer of snow. "Headmaster!" Rowan said again, surging forward after him.

Leith sprang to his feet and halted the boy with his arm. "Wait," he advised.

"He's taking the gauntlet! He's getting away!" Rowan said.

"Wait," Leith said.

The army of specters was a horde in the moonlight. Their attention perked at the sight of the gauntlet, and they slowly disbursed to reveal Marisele's wasted figure in the snow. Her aged form had returned, and she lay on her back, dead. Her head was to one side, facing Leith and Rowan, the eye wide and frozen in terror from the monstrosities the spirits had surely shown her. Their tortured madness had stopped her heart, her creased face still warped with fright.

Wickham stood before them and pulled back the sleeve of his robe. Carefully, he slipped the ornate glove over his thin arm, flinching as the spikes sank into his flesh. He grunted from the pain.

"What's he doing? He's going to take control of them!" Rowan blurted, pointing and pushing against Leith's arm.

"Stay back," Leith ordered, shoving him against a tree.

The night lit up with the gauntlet's sparks as it acclimated to its new master. Wickham raised it at the crowd of spirits and chanted a spell that rang out over the woods.

"Censuro Ameliorem," the old man said.

The gauntlet blazed with light, as white rings pulsed outward toward the ghosts, who stared in awe. As it touched them, the spirits shrank and vanished into a cluster of tiny white orbs, as if the stars had come down to settle on the hill. In seconds, they each darted toward the massive shadow of Solemn Woods.

From a distance, the black trees flashed with each arriving orb that seemed to plunge into the ground, where it disappeared. A powerful wind suddenly shook the night, stirring up the snow and whistling over the landscape.

Leith quickly bent down to Kyler, pulled her hood over her head, and lifted her in his arms. He trudged toward the edge of the birches, some of them swaying in the mysterious gale, while the snow leapt about his boots.

"Leith!" Rowan shouted after him.

Leith continued on, reaching the headmaster, who had turned toward Solemn Woods and was watching the spectacle of white flashes through streaks of wind-tossed white hair. The last orb finally vanished, and the wind ceased. A cloud released its grip on the moon, slowly drifting away. The black trees began to shift and change, as the sound of cracking and rumbling shook the ground. Before Leith's eyes, his forest home mutated. The black trees faded to stone-gray, their contorted branches stretching and straightening into fluid, sinuous limbs.

The blue haze dissipated from the ground, and the howling breezes halted in one final, defeated sigh. It was as if the poisonous spirit had been drained, leaving Solemn Woods a tired skeleton, as parched and colorless as the observatory courtyard. Wickham took a deep, satisfied breath as Rowan approached. The old man detached the gauntlet, shutting his eyes tight as he pulled it from his arm. Its light immediately went out, one last spark jumping as he handed it to Rowan.

"You freed them, didn't you?" Rowan asked, staring down at the gauntlet with astonishment. "You lifted the curse."

Wickham pulled out more rags from his robes as the night grew quiet again and wrapped them about his bleeding arm. "Those priests argued against the Necromantis so relentlessly that they became quite an aggravation," he began. "We came to a compromise. The spell would be enacted, but not for eternity. When the time for its end came near, two forces would show themselves: a rogue sorcerer who exhibits both loyalty and rebellion, and a descendant of the priesthood, torn between darkness and light."

"Kyler," Leith guessed.

Wickham nodded. "Her father was one of the priesthood's most virtuous members, but he fell victim to the charms of a beautiful young sorceress from the Order of Shadow. Of course, their union was forbidden, and it was only a matter of time after Kyler was born that they were discovered," he said. "Her father was murdered by a group of radicals shortly before his trial, and her mother fled to the mountains. She gave Kyler up to the Chamber of Shadow and resigned from the Order. Not long after that, she was stabbed to death in Tawdry Cape."

"And the priesthood disbanded," Leith added.

"Yes. Amaleus was short on devotees as it was. Kyler is perhaps the last of that merciful spirit," Wickham said, placing one hand on her hooded head. "And Marisele," he added, looking over to the ground where the witch's corpse had rapidly decayed, leaving only traces of dried bones and scraps of her red robes like artifacts in the snow, "would have been a danger to us all. Those spirits had their vengeance, I can tell you. Now," he said to Leith, tying off the bandages and pulling his sleeve over them, "Rowan and I will take the girl back to the chamber. The Hypnogoths wait for you. I trust you will not let yourself be distracted. . . ." Wickham told him, taking the gauntlet from Rowan and holding it out to Leith.

Leith cautiously handed Kyler's weak form over to Rowan and took the relic from the headmaster. He gave a short bow, a respect he had not paid the Academy in many years.

"I won't be long."

The landscape looked different. Morning brought with it the familiar fog that draped the shoreline and obscured the view of that enchanted island. The broken stone of the chamber wall was cold under Kyler's palm. She gazed out at the hillside that plunged down toward Solemn Woods. The forest was not the black mark it had been for centuries. From a distance, the trees were like a mass of crooked bones, quiet and unmoving as a grave. The dome of the observatory peeked out from the highest of the limbs, a sleeping remnant of a forgotten age. Kyler let the winter wind climb up to meet her. Below, there was a procession of students in purple on their way to the pre-ceremony to honor those who perished during the siege.

Her robes, a tattered, ink-stained brown with emerald trim, bulked at the shoulder from the dressing of her wound. It was still tender and throbbed with a dull ache. Kyler took in a deep, cold breath and closed her eyes against the rising sun. The brown, ribbon-like tresses of her hair were swept back by the breeze. There were slow footsteps behind her on the bastion.

"Headmaster," she said, startled, and bowing as she turned.

"The ceremony will begin soon," Wickham reminded. "You are certain you are well enough to travel afterward?"

"Well enough in body, my lord, but my spirit still suffers," she answered meekly. Her face was pale and melancholy, and the sparkling eyes were dim and shadowed. "I can only pray that you can one day forgive my betrayal."

The old man smiled. "If you can forgive mine, child, then we shall be at a level. I was working at a purpose, but I will not justify my deception. You have been ever faithful to us, Kyler, and were undeserving. It might please you to know," Wickham said, stepping forward to join her at the ledge, "the power of your magic failed all my best predictions. You stumped me, sorceress, evaded my most potent visions," he admitted, the smile still turning up the corners of his long beard.

It was quiet for a moment, the sun's slow crawl lighting up the field in panels of gold. The traditional song of tribute to those lost in battle had begun on the west side of the chamber. A drum thundered slow and deep, the number of beats matching the number of the slain. Kyler looked out over the hillside with a distant longing. Wickham's smile lessened.

"I cannot tell you where he is, Kyler," he said suddenly.

Kyler did not flinch at his words, nor did her eyes leave the hill. "I know, my lord."

"He has not been seen or heard from since he returned the gauntlet. The Academy is asking for another trial. I have assured them that he is successfully avoiding my detection. I think perhaps they will grow tired of hunting him soon enough," Wickham mused, "and abandon the notion completely. It's a shame, though. Imagine what you might accomplish, serving our Orders together."

At this, Kyler looked over at him, searching the old man's care-worn mask of studious reserve with a sudden suspicion. Wickham cleared his throat and turned from the ledge.

"He has comrades from his days of service who will be pleased to see their old brother-at-arms. Leith will not be alone, wherever he is," the headmaster stressed, and offered her his arm. "Come now," he said. "Claim your robes."

Gentilium flowers rained down on the tree-lined corridor. The wide stone steps of the Chamber of Sight were crowded with attendees, the various colors of their robes a mosaic against the background of the falling white blossoms. Music played—a slow, beautiful melody on strings accompanied by a choir. The first Order to receive their awards was the Order of Sight, the tradition always given to the home chamber. Rowan was the first one called forward in recognition of his valor during the siege. Wickham related his deeds to the crowd, before draping him in a new red robe with gold satin trim.

The rest of the graduates crossed the platform one by one at the top of the stairs, approaching Wickham. He took the scarlet frocks from an attendant and ceremoniously draped each after they had recited their Order's oath. The attendees clapped and whistled with enthusiasm over the choir as the students of each Order were presented with new robes. Rowan had joined Kyler near the platform. His own new robe also hid a bulge of bandages at the shoulder, and his face was scratched in two places. He leaned over to speak to her, the gesture of applause proving too painful for either of them to participate.

"Look how careful they are with the white ones," he joked, as the first of the Order of Light was awarded his bright robe.

The young man looked nervous as Wickham placed it around his shoulders, instantly hitching it up to keep the hem from touching the ground. Kyler and Rowan chuckled.

"I'm so proud of you," she told him in a serious tone. "I know that you saved his life. It was a brave and honorable thing you did."

Rowan gave her a gentle smile. "Master Leith is a great sorcerer. I misjudged him. Your turn," he said suddenly, nudging her toward the platform.

Kyler perked up. Wickham was announcing the Order of Shadow, the first black robe in his hands pinched at the shoulders. She became abruptly aware of her own robe, worn brown and faded, the green stripes frayed here and there. Kyler lovingly touched the ink stain on the sleeve, remembering the nights by candlelight at a table piled with scrolls.

Wickham's voice rang out. "The first robe is to be awarded to a young woman who has served our histories and archives most splendidly for many years," he said. "Her magic had eluded us, her power long overlooked and eventually abandoned. At last, it finally reared its head!" Wickham declared candidly. A murmur of laughter followed. Wickham turned to speak directly to Kyler. "From the Book of Amaleus, 'Often the greatest among us are the ones who are reluctant to see themselves as such.'"

It was quiet then, for there were few that knew anything of the old god. Kyler stared at him, perplexed. Rowan took a step and nudged her forward. She stumbled into a stride and met Wickham at the other side. The robe was before her. Its rich, black velvet folds caught the morning sunlight. She faced Wickham and recited the Oath of Shadow:

"May darkness keep my purpose firm while moon and stars may guide. May nightshade serve my fierce pursuits with Nythos at my side."

Wickham moved toward her. Kyler threaded her arms through the sleeves as he placed it over her shoulders. She looked out at the scene before her, a hundred students and sorcerers-at-arms she could now call her fellows, applauding her accomplishment with warm, welcoming faces. The velvet was heavy and soft, sleek on her form. Its new fabric shifted in the light, revealing hues of dark blue and violet.

"Congratulations," Wickham whispered.

The crowd cheered. Rowan produced a loud, piercing whistle from where he stood. Kyler placed her hand over her chest. With a sigh of resolve and quiet recollection, she remembered her amulet was gone. Descending the steps, she joined the others who were admiring their robes, some their new stripes. It was no more her magic or her station that estranged her from them. Kyler had lived an adventure, become a part of history. The world seemed smaller to her now, and she was already craving the edge of danger.

Leith had not left her thoughts.

Rowan escorted Kyler toward the stables. Pherylon was saddled and ready for the journey to the Chamber of Shadow, where she'd been commissioned one last task as a scribe.

"They wish me to document the siege," she explained to him, soothing her horse with gentle murmurs. "The entire history of the prophecy and the undoing of the Necromantis must be recorded. They insist, I'm afraid. After that, they are sending me out on missions," she said.

"And have you changed your mind about the Hypnogoths?" Rowan teased.

Kyler smirked, then shrugged. "They are a treacherous lot," she admitted. "But I find my original opinion of their peculiar nobility still sound."

"Ah, here is your escort," Rowan announced, nodding at a tall oaf of a man with a mound of curly black hair, who led his own spotted horse from the stable. "I trust that arrow wound won't be too much of a bother."

"I assured Headmaster Wickham I could travel alone, but he wouldn't have it," Kyler said. "But I'm happy to have Hanover, nonetheless," she added with a louder voice, then turned to face her escort.

"Kind of you to say, my lady," Hanover replied humbly, with a short, awkward bow. "We'll be needing to head off soon, miss, if we want the daylight," he said, then advanced forward to help her mount.

Rowan stepped back as the big man gingerly supported her weight while she climbed on. Kyler took the reins with natural ease. Pherylon was strangely alert and in good spirits. Hanover turned and bowed again.

"Take care of her," Rowan reminded.

"Of course, sir," the man answered, then climbed onto his horse, taking the straps in one hand and patting the horse's neck with the other.

In that moment, Rowan was seized by a vision. There were several rapid flashes before him, seconds running backward: Hanover's grip gentle on Kyler's waist, the tanned, rugged face as he turned. The burly stable hand was walking toward him with a saddle. His mouth formed words, but Rowan couldn't hear him. Rowan saw the man's hand, brown leather wrapped around his thumb. The world rushed back to him. Hanover was saying goodbye. It was an odd tone for the ungraceful escort: serious, reverent, intelligent—and thankful. Rowan's eyes were fixed on Hanover's hands, the sections of his large fingers strained by several small, ornate silver rings.

"Congratulations on your stripes, Master Rowan," were Hanover's last words.

The man pulled up the hood of his battered gray cloak. The sun was at his back, making a shadow of his face. In the instant before he turned to lead the horses down the trail, Rowan caught the faintest sapphire light from under the hood. They were quickly gone, the clatter of the hooves growing distant over the hill. Rowan stood still, blinking in disbelief.

Abruptly, a voice interrupted.

"Congratulations on your stripes, Master Rowan," said the stable hand, as he rounded the corner with a bucket of feed in his arms. "The colors do you right, if I may be so bold, sir," Hanover remarked with a jerky bow.

Rowan's brows knitted in realization. An instinct urged him to look up at the bastion. Headmaster Wickham stood at the wall, peering down. Rowan found the knowing look on the wise old features. The aged seer nodded his head once. Rowan grinned and nodded back.

"You may, my dear Hanover," he answered. "It's very kind of you to say."

- The End -

ABOUT THE AUTHOR

Wendy Tardieu is a college writing professor and life-long fan of great romance and fantasy stories. Her love for romance and fantasy adventure, along with her MFA in Creative Writing, has inspired her to merge the two genres into fiction that excites the senses as well as the imagination.

CONNECT WITH WENDY TARDIEU

Sign up for Wendy's newsletter at
www. wendytardieu.com/newsletter

To find out more information visit her website:
www.wendytardieu.com

Facebook:
www.facebook.com/Buy-my-Book-Fund-my-Latte-117630031582933

BOOK DISCOUNTS AND SPECIAL DEALS

Sign up for free to get discounts and special deals
on our bestselling books at
www.TCKpublishing.com/bookdeals

www.ingramcontent.com/pod-product-compliance
Lightning Source LLC
Chambersburg PA
CBHW070657100726
47907CB00007B/2246